Ask the Dust

Books by John Fante

THE SAGA OF ARTURO BANDINI

Wait Until Spring, Bandini
The Road to Los Angeles
Ask the Dust
Dreams from Bunker Hill

OTHER WORKS AND COLLECTIONS

Full of Life
The Brotherhood of the Grape
The Wine of Youth: Selected Stories of John Fante
1933 Was a Bad Year
West of Rome
The Big Hunger: Stories 1932–1959
Selected Letters 1932–1981
The John Fante Reader

John Fante

Ask the Dust

A NOVEL

With an Introduction by
Charles Bukowski

AN  BOOK

HARPER**PERENNIAL** ● MODERN**CLASSICS**

NEW YORK ● LONDON ● TORONTO ● SYDNEY

For Joyce, with love

HARPER**PERENNIAL** ● MODERN**CLASSICS**

Archival material in the P.S. section used by permission of Tom Fante and the Estate of John Fante.

Grateful acknowledgment is made to Stephen Cooper for the kind use of his personal archives.

An edition of this book was previously published by Black Sparrow Press.

P.S.™ is a trademark of HarperCollins Publishers.

First Ecco edition published 2002.
First Harper Perennial Modern Classics edition published 2006.

The Library of Congress has catalogued the Ecco edition as follows:

Fante, John, 1909-1983.
Ask the dust.
ISBN 0-87685-443-9 (paper edition)
ISBN 0-87685-444-7 (trade cloth edition)
I. Title.
PZ3.F218As   1979   [PS3511.A594]   813'.5'2   79-22399

   ISBN-10: 0-06-082255-4 (pbk.)
   ISBN-13: 978-0-06-082255-2 (pbk.)

23 24 25 26 27 LBC 34 33 32 31 30

Introduction

I was a young man, starving and drinking and trying to be a writer. I did most of my reading at the downtown L.A. Public Library, and nothing that I read related to me or to the streets or to the people about me. It seemed as if everybody was playing word-tricks, that those who said almost nothing at all were considered excellent writers. Their writing was an admixture of subtlety, craft and form, and it was read and it was taught and it was ingested and it was passed on. It was a comfortable contrivance, a very slick and careful Word-Culture. One had to go back to the pre-Revolution writers of Russia to find any gamble, any passion. There were exceptions but those exceptions were so few that reading them was quickly done, and you were left staring at rows and rows of exceedingly dull books. With centuries to look back on, with all their advantages, the moderns just weren't very good.

I pulled book after book from the shelves. Why didn't anybody say something? Why didn't anybody scream out?

I tried other rooms in the library. The section on Religion was just a vast bog—to me. I got into Philosophy. I found a couple of bitter Germans who cheered me for a while, then that was over. I tried Mathematics but upper Math was just like Religion: it ran right off me. What *I* needed seemed to be absent everywhere.

I tried Geology and found it curious but, finally, non-sustaining.

I found some books on Surgery and I liked the books on Surgery: the words were new and the illustrations were wonderful. I particularly liked and memorized the operation on the mesocolon.

Then I dropped out of Surgery and I was back in the big room with the novelists and short story writers. (When I had enough cheap wine to drink I never went to the library. A library was a good place to be when you had nothing to drink or to eat, and the landlady was looking for you and for the back rent money. In the library at least you had the use of the toilet facilities.) I saw quite a number of other bums in there, most of them asleep on top of their books.

I kept on walking around the big room, pulling the books off the shelves, reading a few lines, a few pages, then putting them back.

Then one day I pulled a book down and opened it, and there it was. I stood for a moment, reading. Then like a man who had found gold in the city dump, I carried the book to a table. The lines rolled easily across the page, there was a flow. Each line had its own energy and was followed by another like it. The very substance of each line gave the page a form, a feeling of something *carved* into it. And here, at last, was a man who was not afraid of emotion. The humour and the pain were intermixed with a superb simplicity. The beginning of that book was a wild and enormous miracle to me.

I had a library card. I checked the book out, took it to my room, climbed into my bed and read it, and I knew long before I had finished that here was a man who had evolved a distinct way of writing. The book was *Ask the Dust* and the author was John Fante. He was to be a lifetime influence on my writing. I finished *Ask the Dust* and looked for other books of Fante's in the library. I found two: *Dago Red* and *Wait Until Spring, Bandini*. They were of the same order, written of and from the gut and the heart.

Yes, Fante had a mighty effect upon me. Not long after reading these books I began living with a woman. She was a worse drunk than I was and we had some violent arguments, and often I would scream at her, "Don't call me a son of a bitch! *I am Bandini, Arturo Bandini!*"

Fante was my god and I knew that the gods should be left alone, one didn't bang at their door. Yet I liked to guess about where he had lived on Angel's Flight and I imagined it possible that he still lived there. Almost every day I walked by and I thought, is that the window Camilla crawled through? And, is that the hotel door? Is that the lobby? I never knew.

39 years later I reread *Ask the Dust*. That is to say, I reread it this year and it still stands, as do Fante's other works, but this one is my favorite because it was my first discovery of the *magic*. There are other books beside *Dago Red* and *Wait Until Spring, Bandini*. They are *Full of Life* and *The Brotherhood of the Grape*. And, at the moment, Fante has a novel in progress, *A Dream of Bunker Hill*.

6

Through other circumstances, I finally met the author this year. There is much more to the story of John Fante. It is a story of terrible luck and a terrible fate and of a rare and natural courage. Some day it will be told but I feel that he doesn't want me to tell it here. But let me say that the way of his words and the way of his way are the same: strong and good and warm.

That's enough. Now this book is yours.

Charles Bukowski
5-6-79

Ask the Dust

Chapter One

One night I was sitting on the bed in my hotel room on Bunker Hill, down in the very middle of Los Angeles. It was an important night in my life, because I had to make a decision about the hotel. Either I paid up or I got out: that was what the note said, the note the landlady had put under my door. A great problem, deserving acute attention. I solved it by turning out the lights and going to bed.

In the morning I awoke, decided that I should do more physical exercise, and began at once. I did several bending exercises. Then I washed my teeth, tasted blood, saw pink on the toothbrush, remembered the advertisements, and decided to go out and get some coffee.

I went to the restaurant where I always went to the restaurant and I sat down on the stool before the long counter and ordered coffee. It tasted pretty much like coffee, but it wasn't worth the nickel. Sitting there I smoked a couple of cigarets, read the box scores of the American League games, scrupulously avoided the box scores of National League games, and noted with satisfaction that Joe DiMaggio was still a credit to the Italian people, because he was leading the league in batting.

A great hitter, that DiMaggio. I walked out of the restaurant, stood before an imaginary pitcher, and swatted a home run over the fence. Then I walked down the street toward Angel's Flight, wondering what I would do that day. But there was nothing to do, and so I decided to walk around the town.

I walked down Olive Street past a dirty yellow apartment house that was still wet like a blotter from last night's fog, and I thought of my friends Ethie and Carl, who were from Detroit and had lived there, and I remembered the night Carl hit Ethie because she was

11

going to have a baby, and he didn't want a baby. But they had the baby and that's all there was to that. And I remembered the inside of that apartment, how it smelled of mice and dust, and the old women who sat in the lobby on hot afternoons, and the old woman with the pretty legs. Then there was the elevator man, a broken man from Milwaukee, who seemed to sneer every time you called your floor, as though you were such a fool for choosing that particular floor, the elevator man who always had a tray of sandwiches in the elevator, and a pulp magazine.

Then I went down the hill on Olive Street, past the horrible frame houses reeking with murder stories, and on down Olive to the Philharmonic Auditorium, and I remembered how I'd gone there with Helen to listen to the Don Cossack Choral Group, and how I got bored and we had a fight because of it, and I remembered what Helen wore that day—a white dress, and how it made me sing at the loins when I touched it. Oh that Helen—but not here.

And so I was down on Fifth and Olive, where the big street cars chewed your ears with their noise, and the smell of gasoline made the sight of the palm trees seem sad, and the black pavement still wet from the fog of the night before.

So now I was in front of the Biltmore Hotel, walking along the line of yellow cabs, with all the cab drivers asleep except the driver near the main door, and I wondered about these fellows and their fund of information, and I remembered the time Ross and I got an address from one of them, how he leered salaciously and then took us to Temple Street, of all places, and whom did we see but two very unattractive ones, and Ross went all the way, but I sat in the parlor and played the phonograph and was scared and lonely.

I was passing the doorman of the Biltmore, and I hated him at once, with his yellow braids and six feet of height and all that dignity, and now a black automobile drove to the curb, and a man got out. He looked rich; and then a woman got out, and she was beautiful, her fur was silver fox, and she was a song across the sidewalk and inside the swinging doors, and I thought oh boy for a little of that, just a day and a night of that, and she was a dream as I walked along, her perfume still in the wet morning air.

Then a great deal of time passed as I stood in front of a pipe shop and looked, and the whole world faded except that window and I stood and smoked them all, and saw myself a great author with that natty Italian briar, and a cane, stepping out of a big black car, and she was there too, proud as hell of me, the lady in the silver fox fur. We registered and then we had cocktails and then we danced awhile, and then we had another cocktail and I recited some lines from Sanskrit, and the world was so wonderful, because every two minutes some gorgeous one gazed at me, the great author, and nothing would do but I had to autograph her menu, and the silver fox girl was very jealous.

Los Angeles, give me some of you! Los Angeles come to me the way I came to you, my feet over your streets, you pretty town I loved you so much, you sad flower in the sand, you pretty town.

A day and another day and the day before, and the library with the big boys in the shelves, old Dreiser, old Mencken, all the boys down there, and I went to see them, Hya Dreiser, Hya Mencken, Hya, hya: there's a place for me, too, and it begins with B, in the B shelf, Arturo Bandini, make way for Arturo Bandini, his slot for his book, and I sat at the table and just looked at the place where my book would be, right there close to Arnold Bennett; not much that Arnold Bennett, but I'd be there to sort of bolster up the B's, old Arturo Bandini, one of the boys, until some girl came along, some scent of perfume through the fiction room, some click of high heels to break up the monotony of my fame. Gala day, gala dream!

But the landlady, the white-haired landlady kept writing those notes: she was from Bridgeport, Connecticut, her husband had died and she was all alone in the world and she didn't trust any-body, she couldn't afford to, she told me so, and she told me I'd have to pay. It was mounting like the national debt, I'd have to pay or leave, every cent of it—five weeks overdue, twenty dollars, and if I didn't she'd hold my trunks; only I didn't have any trunks, I only had a suitcase and it was cardboard without even a strap, be-cause the strap was around my belly holding up my pants, and that wasn't much of a job, because there wasn't much left of my pants.

"I just got a letter from my agent," I told her. "My agent in New York. He says I sold another one; he doesn't say where, but he says he's got one sold. So don't worry Mrs. Hargraves, don't you fret, I'll have it in a day or so."

But she couldn't believe a liar like me. It wasn't really a lie; it was a wish, not a lie, and maybe it wasn't even a wish, maybe it was a fact, and the only way to find out was watch the mailman, watch him closely, check his mail as he laid it on the desk in the lobby, ask him point blank if he had anything for Bandini. But I didn't have to ask after six months at that hotel. He saw me coming and he always nodded yes or no before I asked: no, three million times; yes, once.

One day a beautiful letter came. Oh, I got a lot of letters, but this was the only beautiful letter, and it came in the morning, and it said (he was talking about *The Little Dog Laughed*) he had read *The Little Dog Laughed* and liked it; he said, Mr. Bandini, if ever I saw a genius, you are it. His name was Leonardo, a great Italian critic, only he was not known as a critic, he was just a man in West Virginia, but he was great and he was a critic, and he died. He was dead when my airmail letter got to West Virginia, and his sister sent my letter back. She wrote a beautiful letter too, she was a pretty good critic too, telling me Leonardo had died of consumption but he was happy to the end, and one of the last things he did was sit up in bed and write me about *The Little Dog Laughed:* a dream out of life, but very important; Leonardo, dead now, a saint in heaven, equal to any apostle of the twelve.

Everybody in the hotel read *The Little Dog Laughed*, everybody: a story to make you die holding the page, and it wasn't about a dog, either: a clever story, screaming poetry. And the great editor, none but J. C. Hackmuth with his name signed like Chinese said in a letter: a great story and I'm proud to print it. Mrs. Hargraves read it and I was a different man in her eyes thereafter. I got to stay on in that hotel, not shoved out in the cold, only often it was in the heat, on account of *The Little Dog Laughed*. Mrs. Grainger in 345, a Christian Scientist (wonderful hips, but kinda old) from Battle Creek, Michigan, sitting in the lobby waiting to die, and *The Little Dog Laughed* brought her back to the earth, and that look in her eyes made me know it was right and I was right, but I was hoping she would ask about my finances, how I was getting along, and then I thought why not ask her to lend you a five spot, but I didn't and I walked away snapping my fingers in disgust.

The hotel was called the Alta Loma. It was built on a hillside in reverse, there on the crest of Bunker Hill, built against the decline of the hill, so that the main floor was on the level with the street but the tenth floor was downstairs ten levels. If you had room 862, you got in the elevator and went down eight floors, and if you wanted to go down in the truck room, you didn't go down but up to the attic, one floor above the main floor.

Oh for a Mexican girl! I used to think of her all the time, my Mexican girl. I didn't have one, but the streets were full of them, the Plaza and Chinatown were afire with them, and in my fashion they were mine, this one and that one, and some day when another check came it would be a fact. Meanwhile it was free and they were Aztec princesses and Mayan princesses, the peon girls in the Grand Central Market, in the Church of Our Lady, and I even went to Mass to look at them. That was sacrilegious conduct but it was better than not going to Mass at all, so that when I wrote home to Colorado to my mother I could write with truth. Dear Mother: I went to Mass last Sunday. Down in the Grand Central Market I bumped into the princesses accidentally on purpose. It gave me a chance to speak to them, and I smiled and said excuse me. Those beautiful girls, so happy when you acted like a gentleman and all of that, just to touch them and carry the memory of it back to my room, where dust gathered upon my typewriter and Pedro the mouse sat in his hole, his black eyes watching me through that time of dream and reverie.

Pedro the mouse, a good mouse but never domesticated, refusing to be petted or house-broken. I saw him the first time I walked into my room, and that was during my hey-day, when *The Little Dog Laughed* was in the current August issue. It was five months ago, the day I got to town by bus from Colorado with a hundred

15

and fifty dollars in my pocket and big plans in my head. I had a philosophy in those days. I was a lover of man and beast alike, and Pedro was no exception; but cheese got expensive, Pedro called all his friends, the room swarmed with them, and I had to quit it and feed them bread. They didn't like bread. I had spoiled them and they went elsewhere, all but Pedro the ascetic who was content to eat the pages of an old Gideon Bible.

Ah, that first day! Mrs. Hargraves opened the door to my room, and there it was, with a red carpet on the floor, pictures of the English countryside on the walls, and a shower adjoining. The room was down on the sixth floor, room 678, up near the front of the hill, so that my window was on a level with the green hillside and there was no need for a key, for the window was always open. Through that window I saw my first palm tree, not six feet away, and sure enough I thought of Palm Sunday and Egypt and Cleopatra, but the palm was blackish at its branches, stained by carbon monoxide coming out of the Third Street Tunnel, its crusted trunk choked with dust and sand that blew in from the Mojave and Santa Ana deserts.

Dear Mother, I used to write home to Colorado, Dear Mother, things are definitely looking up. A big editor was in town and I had lunch with him and we have signed a contract for a number of short stories, but I won't try to bore you with all the details, dear mother, because I know you're not interested in writing, and I know Papa isn't, but it levels down to a swell contract, only it doesn't begin for a couple of months. So send me ten dollars, mother, send me five, mother dear, because the editor (I'd tell you his name only I know you're not interested in such things) is all set to start me out on the biggest project he's got.

Dear Mother, and Dear Hackmuth, the great editor—they got most of my mail, practically all of my mail. Old Hackmuth with his scowl and his hair parted in the middle, great Hackmuth with a pen like a sword, his picture was on my wall autographed with his signature that looked Chinese. Hya Hackmuth, I used to say, Jesus how you can write! Then the lean days came, and Hackmuth got big letters from me. My God, Mr. Hackmuth, something's wrong with me: the old zip is gone and I can't write anymore. Do you think, Mr. Hackmuth, that the climate here has anything to do with it? Please advise. Do you think, Mr. Hackmuth, that I write as well as William Faulkner? Please advise. Do you think, Mr. Hackmuth, that sex has anything to do with it, because, Mr. Hackmuth, because, because, and I told Hackmuth everything. I told him about the blonde girl I met in the park. I told him how I worked it, how the blonde girl tumbled. I told him the whole story, only it wasn't true, it was a crazy lie—but it was something. It was writing, keeping in touch with the great, and he always answered. Oh boy, he was swell! He answered right off, a great man responding to the problems of a man of talent. Nobody got that many letters from Hackmuth, nobody but me, and I used to take them out and read them over, and kiss them. I'd stand before Hackmuth's picture crying out of both eyes, telling him he picked a good one this time, a great one, a Bandini, Arturo Bandini, me.

The lean days of determination. That was the word for it, determination: Arturo Bandini in front of his typewriter two full days in succession, determined to succeed; but it didn't work, the longest siege of hard and fast determination in his life, and not one line done, only two words written over and over across the page, up and down, the same words: palm tree, palm tree, palm tree, a battle to the death between the palm tree and me, and the palm tree won: see it out there swaying in the blue air, creaking sweetly in the blue air. The palm tree won after two fighting days, and I crawled out of the window and sat at the foot of the tree. Time passed, a moment or two, and I slept, little brown ants carousing in the hair on my legs.

Chapter Two

I was twenty then. What the hell, I used to say, take your time, Bandini. You got ten years to write a book, so take it easy, get out and learn about life, walk the streets. That's your trouble: your ignorance of life. Why, my God, man, do you realize you've never had any experience with a woman? Oh yes I have, oh I've had plenty. Oh no you haven't. You need a woman, you need a bath, you need a good swift kick, you need money. They say it's a dollar, they say it's two dollars in the swell places, but down on the Plaza it's a dollar; swell, only you haven't got a dollar, and another thing, you coward, even if you had a dollar you wouldn't go, because you had a chance to go once in Denver and you didn't. No, you coward, you were afraid, and you're still afraid, and you're glad you haven't got a dollar.

Afraid of a woman! Ha, great writer this! How can he write about women, when he's never had a woman? Oh you lousy fake, you phony, no wonder you can't write! No wonder there wasn't a woman in *The Little Dog Laughed*. No wonder it wasn't a love story, you fool, you dirty little schoolboy.

To write a love story, to learn about life.

Money arrived in the mail. Not a check from the mighty Hackmuth, not an acceptance from *The Atlantic Monthly* or *The Saturday Evening Post*. Only ten dollars, only a fortune. My mother sent it: some dime insurance policies, Arturo, I had them taken up for their cash value, and this is your share. But it was ten dollars; one manuscript or another, at least something had been sold.

Put it in your pocket, Arturo. Wash your face, comb your hair, put some stuff on to make you smell good while you stare into the mirror looking for grey hairs; because you're worried Arturo,

18

you're worried, and that brings grey hair. But there was none, not a strand. Yeah, but what of that left eye? It looked discolored. Careful, Arturo Bandini: don't strain your eyesight, remember what happened to Tarkington, remember what happened to James Joyce.

Not bad, standing in the middle of the room, talking to Hackmuth's picture, not bad, Hackmuth, you'll get a story out of this. How do I look, Hackmuth? Do you sometimes wonder, Herr Hackmuth, what I look like? Do you sometimes say to yourself, I wonder if he's handsome, that Bandini fellow, author of that brilliant *Little Dog Laughed?*

Once in Denver there was another night like this, only I was not an author in Denver, but I stood in a room like this and made these plans, and it was disastrous because all the time in that place I thought about the Blessed Virgin and *thou shalt not commit adultery* and the hard-working girl shook her head sadly and had to give it up, but that was a long time ago and tonight it will be changed.

I climbed out the window and scaled the incline to the top of Bunker Hill. A night for my nose, a feast for my nose, smelling the stars, smelling the flowers, smelling the desert, and the dust asleep, across the top of Bunker Hill. The city spread out like a Christmas tree, red and green and blue. Hello, old houses, beautiful hamburgers singing in cheap cafes, Bing Crosby singing too. She'll treat me gently. Not those girls of my childhood, those girls of my boyhood, those girls of my university days. They frightened me, they were diffident, they refused me; but not my princess, because she will understand. She, too, has been scorned.

Bandini, walking along, not tall but solid, proud of his muscles, squeezing his fist to revel in the hard delight of his biceps, absurdly fearless Bandini, fearing nothing but the unknown in a world of mysterious wonder. Are the dead restored? The books say no, the night shouts yes. I am twenty, I have reached the age of reason, I am about to wander the streets below, seeking a woman. Is my soul already smirched, should I turn back, does an angel watch over me, do the prayers of my mother allay my fears, do the prayers of my mother annoy me?

Ten dollars: it will pay the rent for two and a half weeks, it will buy me three pairs of shoes, two pair of pants, or one thousand postage stamps to send material to the editors; indeed! But you haven't any material, your talent is dubious, your talent is pitiful, you haven't any talent, and stop lying to yourself day after day because you know *The Little Dog Laughed* is no good, and it will always be no good.

So you walk along Bunker Hill, and you shake your fist at the sky, and I know what you're thinking, Bandini. The thoughts of your father before you, lash across your back, hot fire in your skull, that you are not to blame: this is your thought, that you were born poor, son of miseried peasants, driven because you were poor, fled from your Colorado town because you were poor, rambling the gutters of Los Angeles because you are poor, hoping to write a book to get rich, because those who hated you back there in Colorado will not hate you if you write a book. You are a coward, Bandini, a traitor to your soul, a feeble liar before your weeping Christ. This is why you write, this is why it would be better if you died.

Yes, it's true: but I have seen houses in Bel-Air with cool lawns and green swimming pools. I have wanted women whose very shoes are worth all I have ever possessed. I have seen golf clubs on Sixth Street in the Spalding window that make me hungry just to grip them. I have grieved for a necktie like a holy man for indulgences. I have admired hats in Robinson's the way critics gasp at Michelangelo.

I took the steps down Angel's Flight to Hill Street: a hundred and forty steps, with tight fists, frightened of no man, but scared of the Third Street Tunnel, scared to walk through it—claustrophobia. Scared of high places too, and of blood, and of earthquakes; otherwise, quite fearless, excepting death, except the fear I'll scream in a crowd, except the fear of appendicitis, except the fear of heart trouble, even that, sitting in his room holding the clock and pressing his jugular vein, counting out his heartbeats, listening to the weird purr and whirr of his stomach. Otherwise, quite fearless.

Here is an idea with money: these steps, the city below, the stars within throwing distance: boy meets girl idea, good setup, big money idea. Girl lives in that grey apartment house, boy is a wanderer. Boy—he's me. Girl's hungry. Rich Pasadena girl hates money. Deliberately left Pasadena millions 'cause of ennui, weariness with money. Beautiful girl, gorgeous. Great story, pathological conflict. Girl with money phobia: Freudian setup. Another guy loves her, rich guy. I'm poor. I meet rival. Beat him to death with caustic wit and also lick him with fists. Girl impressed, falls for me. Offers me millions. I marry her on condition she'll stay poor. Agrees. But ending happy: girl tricks me with huge trust fund day we get married. I'm indignant but I forgive her 'cause I love her. Good idea, but something missing: Collier's story.

Dearest Mother, thanks for the ten dollar bill. My agent announces the sale of another story, this time to a great magazine in London, but it seems they do not pay until publication, and so your little sum will come in handy for various odds and ends.

I went to the burlesque show. I had the best seat possible, a dollar and ten cents, right under a chorus of forty frayed bottoms: some day all of these will be mine: I will own a yacht and we will go on South Sea Cruises. On warm afternoons they will dance for me on the sun deck. But mine will be beautiful women, selections from the cream of society, rivals for the joys of my stateroom. Well, this is good for me, this is experience, I am here for a reason, these moments run into pages, the seamy side of life.

Then Lola Linton came on, slithering like a satin snake amid the tumult of whistling and pounding feet, Lola Linton lascivious, slithering and looting my body, and when she was through, my teeth ached from my clamped jaws and I hated the dirty lowbrow swine around me, shouting their share of a sick joy that belonged to me.

If Mamma sold the policies things must be tough for the Old Man and I shouldn't be here. When I was a kid pictures of Lola Lintons used to come my way, and I used to get so impatient with the slow crawl of time and boyhood, longing for this very moment, and here I am, and I have not changed nor have the Lola Lintons, but I fashioned myself rich and I am poor.

Main Street after the show, midnight: neon tubes and a light fog, honky tonks and all night picture houses. Secondhand stores and Filipino dance halls, cocktails 15¢, continuous entertainment, but I had seen them all, so many times, spent so much Colorado money in them. It left me lonely like a thirsty man holding a cup, and I walked toward the Mexican Quarter with a feeling of sickness without pain. Here was the Church of Our Lady, very old, the adobe blackened with age. For sentimental reasons I will go inside. For sentimental reasons only. I have not read Lenin, but I have heard him quoted, religion is the opium of the people. Talking to myself on the church steps: yeah, the opium of the people. Myself, I am an atheist: I have read *The Anti-Christ* and I regard it as a capital piece of work. I believe in the transvaluation of values, Sir. The Church must go, it is the haven of the booboisie, of boobs and bounders and all brummagem mountebanks.

I pulled the huge door open and it gave a little cry like weeping. Above the altar sputtered the blood-red eternal light, illuminating in crimson shadow the quiet of almost two thousand years. It was like death, but I could remember screaming infants at baptism too. I knelt. This was habit, this kneeling. I sat down. Better to kneel, for the sharp bite at the knees was a distraction from the awful quiet. A prayer. Sure, one prayer: for sentimental reasons. Almighty God, I am sorry I am now an atheist, but have You read Nietzsche? Ah, such a book! Almighty God, I will play fair in this. I will make You a proposition. Make a great writer out of me, and I will return to the Church. And please, dear God, one more favor: make my mother happy. I don't care about the Old Man; he's got his wine and his health, but my mother worries so. Amen.

I closed the weeping door and stood on the steps, the fog like a huge white animal everywhere, the Plaza like our courthouse back home, snowbound in white silence. But all sounds traveled swift and sure through the heaviness, and the sound I heard was the click of high heels. A girl appeared. She wore an old green coat, her face molded in a green scarf tied under the chin. On the stairs stood Bandini.

"Hello, honey," she said, smiling, as though Bandini were her husband, or her lover. Then she came to the first step and looked up at him. "How about it, honey? Want me to show you a good time?"

Bold lover, bold and brazen Bandini.

"Nah," he said. "No thanks. Not tonight."

He hurried away, leaving her looking after him, speaking words he lost in flight. He walked half a block. He was pleased. At least she had asked him. At least she had identified him as a man. He whistled a tune from sheer pleasure. Man about town has universal experience. Noted writer tells of night with woman of the streets. Arturo Bandini, famous writer, reveals experience with Los Angeles prostitute. Critics acclaim book finest written.

Bandini (being interviewed prior to departure for Sweden): "My advice to all young writers is quite simple. I would caution them never to evade a new experience. I would urge them to live life in the raw, to grapple with it bravely, to attack it with naked fists."

Reporter: "Mr. Bandini, how did you come to write this book which won you the Nobel Award?"

Bandini: "The book is based on a true experience which happened to me one night in Los Angeles. Every word of that book is true. I lived that book, I experienced it."

Enough. I saw it all. I turned and walked back toward the church. The fog was impenetrable. The girl was gone. I walked on: perhaps I could catch up with her. At the corner I saw her again. She stood talking to a tall Mexican. They walked, crossed the street and entered the Plaza. I followed. My God, a Mexican! Women like that should draw the color line. I hated him, the Spick, the Greaser. They walked under the banana trees in the Plaza, their feet echoing in the fog. I heard the Mexican laugh. Then the girl laughed. They crossed the street and walked down an alley that was the entrance to Chinatown. The oriental neon signs made the fog pinkish. At a rooming house next door to a chop suey restaurant they turned and climbed the stairs. Across the street upstairs a dance was in progress. Along the little street on both sides yellow cabs were parked. I leaned against the front fender of the cab in front of the rooming house and waited. I lit a cigaret and waited. Until hell freezes over, I will wait. Until God strikes me dead, I will wait.

A half hour passed. There were sounds on the steps. The door opened. The Mexican appeared. He stood in the fog, lit a cigaret, and yawned. Then he smiled absently, shrugged, and walked away, the fog swooping upon him. Go ahead and smile. You stinking Greaser—what have you got to smile about? You come from a bashed and a busted race, and just because you went to the room with one of our white girls, you smile. Do you think you would have had a chance, had I accepted on the church steps?

A moment later the steps sounded to the slick of her heels, and the girl stepped into the fog. The same girl, the same green coat, the same scarf. She saw me and smiled. "Hello, honey. Wanna have a good time?"

Easy now, Bandini.

"Oh," I said. "Maybe. And maybe not. Whatcha got?"

"Come up and see, honey."

Stop sniggering, Arturo. Be suave.

"I might come up," I said. "And then, I might not."

"Aw honey, come on." The thin bones of her face, the odor of sour wine from her mouth, the awful hypocrisy of her sweetness, the hunger for money in her eyes.

Bandini speaking: "What's the price these days?"

She took my arm, pulled me toward the door, but gently.

"You come on up, honey. We'll talk about it up there."

"I'm really not very hot," said Bandini. "I—I just came from a wild party."

Hail Mary full of grace, walking up the stairs, I can't go through with it. I've got to get out of it. The halls smelling of cockroaches, a yellow light at the ceiling, you're too aesthetic for all this, the girl holding my arm, there's something wrong with you, Arturo Bandini, you're a misanthrope, your whole life is doomed to celibacy, you should have been a priest, Father O'Leary talking that afternoon, telling us the joys of denial, and my own mother's money too, Oh Mary conceived without sin, pray for us who have recourse to thee—until we got to the top of the stairs and walked down a dusty dark hall to a room at the end, where she turned out the light and we were inside.

A room smaller than mine, carpetless, without pictures, a bed, a table, a wash-stand. She took off her coat. There was a blue print dress underneath. She was bare-legged. She took off the scarf. She was not a real blonde. Black hair grew at the roots. Her nose was crooked slightly. Bandini on the bed, put himself there with an air of casualness, like a man who knew how to sit on a bed.

Bandini: "Nice place you got here."

My God I got to get out of here, this is terrible.

The girl sat beside me, put her arms around me, pushed her breasts against me, kissed me, flecked my teeth with a cold tongue. I jumped to my feet. Oh think fast, my mind, dear mind of mine please get me out of this and it will never happen again. From now on I will return to my Church. Beginning this day my life shall run like sweet water.

The girl lay back, her hands behind her neck, her legs over the bed. I shall smell lilacs in Connecticut, no doubt, before I die, and see the clean white small reticent churches of my youth, the pasture bars I broke to run away.

"Look," I said. "I want to talk to you."

She crossed her legs.

"I'm a writer," I said. "I'm gathering material for a book."

"I knew you were a writer," she said. "Or a business man, or something. You look spiritual, honey."

"I'm a writer, see. I like you and all that. You're okay, I like you. But I want to talk to you, first."

She sat up.

"Haven't you any money, honey?"

Money—ho. And I pulled it out, a small thick roll of dollar bills. Sure I got money, plenty of money, this is a drop in the bucket, money is no object, money means nothing to me.

"What do you charge?"

"It's two dollars, honey."

Then give her three, peel it off easily, like it was nothing at all, smile and hand it to her because money is no object, there's more where this came from, at this moment Mamma sits by the window holding her rosary, waiting for the Old Man to come home, but there's money, there's always money.

She took the money and slipped it under the pillow. She was grateful and her smile was different now. The writer wanted to talk. How were conditions these days? How did she like this kind of life? Oh, come on honey, let's not talk, let's get down to business. No, I want to talk to you, this is important, new book, material. I do this often. How did you ever get into this racket. Oh honey, Chrissakes, you going to ask me that too? But money is no object, I tell you. But my time is valuable, honey. Then here's a couple more bucks. That makes five, my God, five bucks and I'm not out of here yet, how I hate you, you filthy. But you're cleaner than me because you've got no mind to sell, just that poor flesh.

She was overwhelmed, she would do anything. I could have it any way I wanted it, and she tried to pull me to her, but no, let's wait awhile. I tell you I want to talk to you, I tell you money is no object, here's three more, that makes eight dollars, but it doesn't matter. You just keep that eight bucks and buy yourself something nice. And then I snapped my fingers like a man remembering something, something important, an engagement.

"Say!" I said. "That reminds me. What time is it?"

Her chin was at my neck, stroking it. "Don't you worry about the time, honey. You can stay all night."

A man of importance, ah yes, now I remembered, my publisher, he was getting in tonight by plane. Out at Burbank, away out in Burbank. Have to grab a cab and taxi out there, have to hurry. Goodbye, goodbye, you keep that eight bucks, you buy yourself something nice, goodbye, goodbye, running down the stairs, running away, the welcome fog in the doorway below, you keep that eight bucks, oh sweet fog I see you and I'm coming, you clean air, you wonderful world, I'm coming to you, goodbye, yelling up the stairs, I'll see you again, you keep that eight dollars and buy yourself something nice. Eight dollars pouring out of my eyes, Oh Jesus kill me dead and ship my body home, kill me dead and make me die like a pagan fool with no priest to absolve me, no extreme unction, eight dollars, eight dollars. . . .

Chapter Three

The lean days, blue skies with never a cloud, a sea of blue day after day, the sun floating through it. The days of plenty—plenty of worries, plenty of oranges. Eat them in bed, eat them for lunch, push them down for dinner. Oranges, five cents a dozen. Sunshine in the sky, sun juice in my stomach. Down at the Japanese market he saw me coming, that bullet-faced smiling Japanese, and he reached for a paper sack. A generous man, he gave me fifteen, sometimes twenty for a nickel.

"You like banana?" Sure, so he gave me a couple of bananas. A pleasant innovation, orange juice and bananas. "You like apple?" Sure, so he gave me some apples. Here was something new: oranges and apples. "You like peaches?" Indeed, and I carried the brown sack back to my room. An interesting innovation, peaches and oranges. My teeth tore them to pulp, the juices skewering and whimpering at the bottom of my stomach. It was so sad down there in my stomach. There was much weeping, and little gloomy clouds of gas pinched my heart.

My plight drove me to the typewriter. I sat before it, overwhelmed with grief for Arturo Bandini. Sometimes an idea floated harmlessly through the room. It was like a small white bird. It meant no ill-will. It only wanted to help me, dear little bird. But I would strike at it, hammer it out across the keyboard, and it would die on my hands.

What could be the matter with me? When I was a boy I had prayed to St. Teresa for a new fountain pen. My prayer was answered. Anyway, I did get a new fountain pen. Now I prayed to St. Teresa again. Please, sweet and lovely saint, gimme an idea. But she has deserted me, all the gods have deserted me, and like Huysmans I stand alone, my fists clenched, tears in my eyes. If someone only loved me, even a bug, even a mouse, but that too belonged to the past; even Pedro had forsaken me now that the best I could offer him was orange peel.

I thought of home, of spaghetti swimming in rich tomato sauce, smothered in Parmesan cheese, of Mamma's lemon pies, of lamb roasts and hot bread, and I was so miserable that I deliberately sank my fingernails into the flesh of my arm until a spot of blood appeared. It gave me great satisfaction. I was God's most miserable creature, forced even to torturing myself. Surely upon this earth no grief was greater than mine.

Hackmuth must hear of this, mighty Hackmuth, who fostered genius in the pages of his magazine. Dear Mr. Hackmuth, I wrote, describing the glorious past, dear Hackmuth, page upon page, the sun a ball of fire in the West, slowly strangling in a fog bank rising off the coast.

There was a knock on my door, but I remained quiet because it might be that woman after her lousy rent. Now the door opened and a bald, bony, bearded face appeared. It was Mr. Hellfrick, who lived next door. Mr. Hellfrick was an atheist, retired from the army, living on a meager pension, scarcely enough to pay his liquor bills, even though he purchased the cheapest gin on the market. He lived perpetually in a grey bathrobe without a cord or button, and though he made a pretense at modesty he really didn't care, so that his bathrobe was always open and you saw much hair and bones underneath. Mr. Hellfrick had red eyes because every afternoon when the sun hit the west side of the hotel, he slept with his head out the window, his body and legs inside. He had owed me fifteen cents since my first day at the hotel, but after many futile attempts to collect it, I had given up hope of ever possessing the money again. This had caused a breach between us, so I was surprised when his head appeared inside my door.

He squinted secretively, pressed a finger to his lips, and shhhhhhhhhed me to be quiet, even though I hadn't said a word. I wanted him to know my hostility, to remind him that I had no respect for a man who failed to meet his obligations. Now he closed the door quietly and tiptoed across the room on his bony toes, his bathrobe wide open.

"Do you like milk?" he whispered.

I certainly did, and I told him so. Then he revealed his plan. The man who drove the Alden milk route on Bunker Hill was a friend of his. Every morning at four this man parked his milk truck behind the hotel and came up the back stairs to Hellfrick's room for a drink of gin. "And so," he said, "if you like milk, all you have to do is help yourself."

I shook my head.

"That's pretty contemptible, Hellfrick," and I wondered at the friendship between Hellfrick and the milkman. "If he's your friend, why do you have to steal the milk? He drinks your gin. Why don't you ask him for milk?"

"But I don't drink milk," Hellfrick said. "I'm doing this for you."

This looked like an attempt to squirm out of the debt he owed me. I shook my head. "No thanks, Hellfrick. I like to consider myself an honest man."

He shrugged, pulled the bathrobe around him.

"Okay, kid. I was only trying to do you a favor."

I continued my letter to Hackmuth, but I began to taste milk almost immediately. After a while I could not bear it. I lay on the bed in the semi-darkness, allowing myself to be tempted. In a little while all resistance was gone, and I knocked on Hellfrick's door. His room was madness, pulp western magazines over the floor, a bed with sheets blackened, clothes strewn everywhere, and clothes-hooks on the wall conspicuously naked, like broken teeth in a skull. There were dishes on the chairs, cigaret butts pressed out on the window sills. His room was like mine except that he had a small gas stove in one corner and shelves for pots and pans. He got a special rate from the landlady, so that he did his own cleaning and made his own bed, except that he did neither. Hellfrick sat in a rocking chair in his bathrobe, gin bottles around his feet. He was drinking from a bottle in his hand. He was always drinking, day and night, but he never got drunk.

"I've changed my mind," I told him.

He filled his mouth with gin, rolled the liquor around in his cheeks, and swallowed ecstatically. "It's a cinch," he said. Then he got to his feet and crossed the room toward his pants, which lay sprawled out. For a moment I thought he was going to pay back the money he owed me, but he did no more than fumble mysteriously through the pockets, and then he returned empty handed to the chair. I stood there.

"That reminds me," I said. "I wonder if you could pay the money I loaned you."

"Haven't got it," he said.

"Could you pay me a portion of it—say ten cents?"

He shook his head.

"A nickel?"

"I'm broke, kid."

Then he took another swig. It was a fresh bottle, almost full.

"I can't give you any hard cash, kid. But I'll see that you get all the milk you need." Then he explained. The milkman would arrive around four. I was to stay awake and listen for his knock. Hellfrick would keep the milkman occupied for at least twenty minutes. It was a bribe, a means of escaping payment of the debt, but I was hungry.

"But you ought to pay your debts, Hellfrick. You'd be in a bad spot if I was charging you interest."

"I'll pay you, kid," he said. "I'll pay every last penny, just as soon as I can."

I walked back to my room, slamming Hellfrick's door angrily. I didn't wish to seem cruel about the matter, but this was going too far. I knew the gin he drank cost him at least thirty cents a pint. Surely he could control his craving for alcohol long enough to pay his just debts.

The night came reluctantly. I sat at the window, rolling some cigarets with rough cut tobacco and squares of toilet paper. This tobacco had been a whim of mine in more prosperous times. I had bought a can of it, and the pipe for smoking it had been free, attached to the can by a rubber band. But I had lost the pipe. The tobacco was so coarse it made a poor smoke in regular cigaret papers, but wrapped twice in toilet tissue it was powerful and compact, sometimes bursting into flames.

The night came slowly, first the cool odor of it, and then the darkness. Beyond my window spread the great city, the street lamps, the red and blue and green neon tubes bursting to life like bright night flowers. I was not hungry, there were plenty of oranges under the bed, and that mysterious chortling in the pit of my stomach was nothing more than great clouds of tobacco smoke marooned there, trying frantically to find a way out.

So it had happened at last: I was about to become a thief, a cheap milk-stealer. Here was your flash-in-the-pan genius, your one-story-writer: a thief. I held my head in my hands and rocked back and forth. Mother of God. Headlines in the papers, promising writer caught stealing milk, famous protégé of J. C. Hackmuth haled into court on petty thief charge, reporters swarming around me, flashlights popping, give us a statement, Bandini, how did it happen? Well, fellows, it was like this: you see, I've really got plenty of money, big sales of manuscripts and all that, but I was doing a yarn about a fellow who steals a quart of milk, and I wanted to write from experience, so that's what happened, fellows. Watch for the story in the *Post*, I'm calling it "Milk Thief." Leave me your address and I'll send you all free copies.

But it would not happen that way, because nobody knows Arturo Bandini, and you'll get six months, they'll take you to the city jail and you'll be a criminal, and what'll your mother say? and what'll your father say? and can't you hear those fellows around the filling station in Boulder, Colorado, can't you hear them snickering about the great writer caught stealing a quart of milk? Don't do it, Arturo! If you've got an ounce of decency in you, don't do it!

I rose from the chair and paced up and down. Almighty God, give me strength! Hold back this criminal urge! Then, all at once, the whole plan seemed cheap and silly, for at that moment I thought of something else to write in my letter to the great Hackmuth, and for two hours I wrote, until my back ached. When I looked out of my window to the big clock on the St. Paul Hotel, it was almost eleven. The letter to Hackmuth was a very long one— already I had twenty pages. I read the letter. It seemed silly. I felt the blood in my face from blushes. Hackmuth would think me an idiot for writing such puerile nonsense. Gathering the pages, I tossed them into the wastebasket. Tomorrow was another day, and tomorrow I might get an idea for a short story. Meanwhile I would eat a couple of oranges and go to bed.

They were miserable oranges. Sitting on the bed I dug my nails into their thin skins. My own flesh puckered, my mouth was filled with saliva, and I squinted at the thought of them. When I bit into the yellow pulp it shocked me like a cold shower. Oh Bandini, talking to the reflection in the dresser mirror, what sacrifices you make for your art! You might have been a captain of industry, a merchant prince, a big league ball player, leading hitter in the American League, with an average of .415; but no! Here you are, crawling through the days, a starved genius, faithful to your sacred calling. What courage you possess!

I lay in bed, sleepless in the darkness. Mighty Hackmuth, what would he say to all this? He would applaud, his powerful pen would eulogize me in well-turned phrases. And after all, that letter to Hackmuth wasn't such a bad letter. I got up, dug it from the waste-basket, and re-read it. A remarkable letter, cautiously humored. Hackmuth would find it very amusing. It would impress upon him the fact that I was the selfsame author of *The Little Dog Laughed*. There was a story for you! And I opened a drawer filled with copies of the magazine that contained the story. Lying on the bed I read it again, laughing and laughing at the wit of it, murmuring in amazement that I had written it. Then I took to reading it aloud, with gestures, before the mirror. When I was finished there were tears of delight in my eyes and I stood before the picture of Hackmuth, thanking him for recognizing my genius.

I sat before the typewriter and continued the letter. The night deepened, the pages mounted. Ah, if all writing were as easy as a letter to Hackmuth! The pages piled up, twenty-five, thirty, until I looked down to my navel, where I detected a fleshy ring. The irony of it! I was gaining weight: oranges were filling me out! At once I jumped up and did a number of setting-up exercises. I twisted and writhed and rolled. Sweat flowed and breathing came hard. Thirsty and exhausted, I threw myself on the bed. A glass of cool milk would be fine now.

At that moment I heard a knock on Hellfrick's door. Then Hellfrick's grunt as someone entered. It could be no one but the milkman. I looked at the clock: it was almost four. I dressed quickly: pants, shoes, no socks, and a sweater. The hallway was deserted, sinister in the red light of an old electric bulb. I walked deliberately, without stealth, like a man going to the lavatory down the hall. Two flights of whining, irritable stairs and I was on the ground floor. The red and white Alden milk-truck was parked close to the hotel wall in the moon-drenched alley. I reached into the truck and got two full quart bottles firmly by their necks. They felt cool and delicious in my fist. A moment later I was back in my room, the bottles of milk on the dresser table. They seemed to fill the room. They were like human things. They were so beautiful, so fat and prosperous.

You Arturo! I said, you lucky one! It may be the prayers of your mother, and it may be that God still loves you, in spite of your tampering with atheists, but whatever it is, you're lucky.

For old times' sake, I thought, and for old times' sake I knelt down and said grace, the way we used to do it in grade school, the way my mother taught us back home: Bless us, Oh Lord, and these Thy gifts, which we are about to receive from Thy most bountiful hands, through the same Christ, Our Lord, Amen. And I added another prayer for good measure. Long after the milkman left Hellfrick's room I was still on my knees, a full half hour of prayers, until I was ravenous for the taste of milk, until my knees ached and a dull pain throbbed in my shoulder blades.

When I got up I staggered from cramped muscles, but it was going to be worthwhile. I took the toothbrush from my glass, opened one of the bottles, and poured a full glass. I turned and faced the picture of J. C. Hackmuth on the wall.

"To you, Hackmuth! Hurray for you!"

And I drank, greedily, until my throat suddenly choked and contracted and a horrible taste shook me. It was the kind of milk I hated. It was buttermilk. I spat it out, washed my mouth with water, and hurried to look at the other bottle. It was buttermilk, too.

Chapter Four

Down on Spring Street, in a bar across the street from the second-hand store. With my last nickel I went there for a cup of coffee. An old style place, sawdust on the floor, crudely drawn nudes smeared across the walls. It was a saloon where old men gathered, where the beer was cheap and smelled sour, where the past remained unaltered.

I sat at one of the tables against the wall. I remember that I sat with my head in my hands. I heard her voice without looking up. I remember that she said, "Can I get you something?" and I said something about coffee with cream. I sat there until the cup was before me, a long time I sat like that, thinking of the hopelessness of my fate.

It was very bad coffee. When the cream mixed with it I realized it was not cream at all, for it turned a greyish color, and the taste was that of boiled rags. This was my last nickel, and it made me angry. I looked around for the girl who had waited on me. She was five or six tables away, serving beers from a tray. Her back was to me, and I saw the tight smoothness of her shoulders under a white smock, the faint trace of muscle in her arms, and the black hair so thick and glossy, falling to her shoulders.

At last she turned around and I waved to her. She was only faintly attentive, widening her eyes in an expression of bored aloofness. Except for the contour of her face and the brilliance of her teeth, she was not beautiful. But at that moment she turned to smile at one of her old customers, and I saw a streak of white under her lips. Her nose was Mayan, flat, with large nostrils. Her lips were heavily rouged, with the thickness of a negress' lips. She was a racial type, and as such she was beautiful, but she was too strange for me. Her eyes were at a high slant, her skin was dark but not black, and as she walked her breasts moved in a way that showed their firmness.

She ignored me after that first glance. She went on to the bar, where she ordered more beer and waited for the thin bartender to draw it. As she waited she whistled, looked at me vaguely and went on whistling. I had stopped waving, but I made it plain I wanted her to come to my table. Suddenly she opened her mouth to the ceiling and laughed in a most mysterious fashion, so that even the bartender wondered at her laughter. Then she danced away, swinging the tray gracefully, picking her way through the tables to a group far down in the rear of the saloon. The bartender followed her with his eyes, still confused at her laughter. But I understood her laughter. It was for me. She was laughing at me. There was something about my appearance, my face, my posture, something about me sitting there that had amused her, and as I thought of it I clenched my fists and considered myself with angry humiliation. I touched my hair: it was combed. I fumbled with my collar and tie: they were clean and in place. I stretched myself to the range of the bar mirror, where I saw what was certainly a worried and sallow face, but not a funny face, and I was very angry.

I began to sneer, watched her closely and sneered. She did not approach my table. She moved near it, even to the table adjacent, but she did not venture beyond that. Each time I saw the dark face, the black large eyes flashing their laughter, I set my lips to a curl that meant I was sneering. It became a game. The coffee cooled, grew cold, a scum of milk gathered over the surface, but I did not touch it. The girl moved like a dancer, her strong silk legs gathering bits of sawdust as her tattered shoes glided over the marble floor.

Those shoes, they were huaraches, the leather thongs wrapped several times around her ankles. They were desperately ragged huaraches; the woven leather had become unraveled. When I saw them I was very grateful, for it was a defect about her that deserved criticism. She was tall and straight-shouldered, a girl of perhaps twenty, faultless in her way, except for her tattered huaraches. And so I fastened my stare on them, watched them intently and deliberately, even turning in my chair and twisting my neck to glare at them, sneering and chuckling to myself. Plainly I was getting as much enjoyment out of this as she got from my face, or whatever it was that amused her. This had a powerful effect upon her. Gradually her pirouetting and dancing subsided and she merely hurried back and forth, and at length she was making her way stealthily. She was embarrassed, and once I saw her glance down quickly and examine her feet, so that in a few minutes she no longer laughed; instead, there was a grimness in her face, and finally she was glancing at me with bitter hatred.

Now I was exultant, strangely happy. I felt relaxed. The world was full of uproariously amusing people. Now the thin bartender looked in my direction and I winked a comradely greeting. He tossed his head in an acknowledging nod. I sighed and sat back, at ease with life.

She had not collected the nickel for the coffee. She would have to do so, unless I left it on the table and walked out. But I wasn't going to walk out. I waited. A half hour passed. When she hurried to the bar for more beer, she no longer waited at the rail in plain sight. She walked around to the back of the bar. She didn't look at me anymore, but I knew she knew I watched her.

Finally she walked straight for my table. She walked proudly, her chin tilted, her hands hanging at her sides. I wanted to stare, but I couldn't keep it up. I looked away, smiling all the while.

"Do you want anything else?" she asked.

Her white smock smelled of starch.

"You call this stuff coffee?" I said.

Suddenly she laughed again. It was a shriek, a mad laugh like the clatter of dishes and it was over as quickly as it began. I looked at her feet again. I could feel something inside her retreating. I wanted to hurt her.

"Maybe this isn't coffee at all," I said. "Maybe it's just water after they boiled your filthy shoes in it." I looked up to her black blazing eyes. "Maybe you don't know any better. Maybe you're just naturally careless. But if I were a girl I wouldn't be seen in a Main Street alley with those shoes."

I was panting when I finished. Her thick lips trembled and the fists in her pocket were writhing under the starched stiffness.

"I hate you," she said.

I felt her hatred. I could smell it, even hear it coming out of her, but I sneered again. "I hope so," I said. "Because there must be something pretty fine about a guy who rates your hatred."

Then she said a strange thing; I remember it clearly. "I hope you die of heart failure," she said. "Right there in that chair."

It gave her keen satisfaction, even though I laughed. She walked away smiling. She stood at the bar again, waiting for more beer, and her eyes were fastened on me, brilliant with her strange wish, and I was uncomfortable but still laughing. Now she was dancing again, gliding from table to table with her tray, and every time I looked at her she smiled her wish, until it had a mysterious effect on me, and I became conscious of my inner organism, of the beat of my heart and the flutter of my stomach. I felt that she would not come back to my table again, and I remember that I was glad of it, and that a strange restlessness came over me, so that I was anxious to get away from that place, and away from the range of her persistent smile. Before I left I did something that pleased me very much. I took the five cents from my pocket and placed it on the table. Then I spilled half the coffee over it. She would have to mop up the mess with her towel. The brown ugliness spread everywhere over the table, and as I got up to leave it was trickling to the floor. At the door I paused to look at her once more. She smiled the same smile. I nodded at the spilled coffee. Then I tossed my fingers in a salute of farewell and walked into the street. Once more I had a good feeling. Once more it was as before, the world was full of amusing things.

I don't remember what I did after I left her. Maybe I went up to Benny Cohen's room over the Grand Central Market. He had a wooden leg with a little door in it. Inside the door were marijuana cigarets. He sold them for fifteen cents apiece. He also sold newspapers, the *Examiner* and the *Times*. He had a room piled high with copies of *The New Masses*. Maybe he saddened me as always with his grim horrible vision of the world tomorrow. Maybe he poked his stained fingers under my nose and cursed me for betraying the proletariat from which I came. Maybe, as always, he sent me trembling out of his room and down the dusty stairs to the fog-dimmed street, my fingers itching for the throat of an imperialist. Maybe, and maybe not; I don't remember.

But I remember that night in my room, the lights of the St. Paul Hotel throwing red and green blobs across my bed as I lay and shuddered and dreamed of the anger of that girl, of the way she danced from table to table, and the black glance of her eyes. That I remember, even to forgetting I was poor and without an idea for a story.

I looked for her early the next morning. Eight o'clock, and I was down on Spring Street. I had a copy of *The Little Dog Laughed* in my pocket. She would think differently about me if she read that story. I had it autographed, right there in my back pocket, ready to present at the slightest notice. But the place was closed at that early hour. It was called the Columbia Buffet. I pushed my nose against the window and looked inside. The chairs were piled upon the tables, and an old man in rubber boots was swabbing the floor. I walked down the street a block or two, the wet air already bluish from monoxide gas. A fine idea came into my head. I took out the magazine and erased the autograph. In its place I wrote, "To a Mayan Princess, from a worthless Gringo." This seemed right, exactly the correct spirit. I walked back to the Columbia Buffet and pounded the front window. The old man opened the door with wet hands, sweat seeping from his hair.

I said, "What's the name of that girl who works here?"

"You mean Camilla?"

"The one who worked here last night."

"That's her," he said. "Camilla Lopez."

"Will you give this to her?" I said. "Just give it to her. Tell her a fellow came by and said for you to give it to her."

He wiped his dripping hands on his apron and took the magazine. "Take good care of it," I said. "It's valuable."

The old man closed the door. Through the glass I saw him limp back to his mop and bucket. He placed the magazine on the bar and resumed his work. A little breeze flipped the pages of the magazine. As I walked away I was afraid he would forget all about it. When I reached the Civic Center I realized I had made a bad mistake: the inscription on the story would never impress that kind of a girl. I hurried back to the Columbia Buffet and banged the window with my knuckles. I heard the old man grumbling and swearing as he fumbled with the lock. He wiped the sweat from his old eyes and saw me again.

"Could I have that magazine?" I said. "I want to write something in it."

The old man couldn't understand any of this. He shook his head with a sigh and told me to come inside. "Go get it yourself, god-damnit," he said. "I got work to do."

I flattened the magazine on the bar and erased the inscription to the Mayan Princess. In place of it I wrote:

Dear Ragged Shoes,
You may not know it, but last night you insulted the au-
thor of this story. Can you read? If so, invest fifteen min-
utes of your time and treat yourself to a masterpiece.
And next time, be careful. Not everyone who comes into
this dive is a bum.

Arturo Bandini

I handed the magazine to the old man, but he did not lift his eyes from his work. "Give this to Miss Lopez," I said. "And see to it that she gets it personally."

The old man dropped the mop handle, smeared the sweat from his wrinkled face, and pointed at the front door. "You get out of here!" he said.

I laid the magazine on the bar again and strolled away leisurely. At the door I turned and waved.

Chapter Five

I wasn't starving. I still had some old oranges under the bed. That night I ate three or four and with the darkness I walked down Bunker Hill to the downtown district. Across the street from the Columbia Buffet I stood in a shadowed doorway and watched Camilla Lopez. She was the same, dressed in the same white smock. I trembled when I saw her and a strange hot feeling was in my throat. But after a few minutes the strangeness was gone and I stood in the darkness until my feet ached.

When I saw a policeman strolling toward me I walked away. It was a hot night. Sand from the Mojave had blown across the city. Tiny brown grains of sand clung to my fingertips whenever I touched anything, and when I got back to my room I found the mechanism of my new typewriter glutted with sand. It was in my ears and in my hair. When I took off my clothes it fell like powder to the floor. It was even between the sheets of my bed. Lying in the darkness, the red light from the St. Paul Hotel flashing on and off across my bed was bluish now, a ghastly color jumping into the room and out again.

I couldn't eat any oranges the next morning. The thought of them made me wince. By noon, after an aimless walk downtown, I was sick with self-pity, unable to control my grief. When I got back to my room I threw myself on the bed and wept from deep inside my chest. I let it flow from every part of me, and after I could not cry anymore I felt fine again. I felt truthful and clean. I sat down and wrote my mother an honest letter. I told her I had been lying to her for weeks; and please send some money, because I wanted to come home.

As I wrote Hellfrick entered. He was wearing pants and no bathrobe, and at first I didn't recognize him. Without a word he put fifteen cents on the table. "I'm an honest man, kid," he said. "I'm as honest as the day is long." And he walked out.

I brushed the coins into my hand, jumped out the window and ran down the street to the grocery store. The little Japanese had his sack ready at the orange bin. He was amazed to see me pass him by and enter the staples department. I bought two dozen cookies. Sitting on the bed I swallowed them as fast as I could, washing them down with gulps of water. I felt fine again. My stomach was full, and I still had a nickel left. I tore up the letter to my mother and lay down to wait for the night. That nickel meant I could go back to the Columbia Buffet. I waited, heavy with food, heavy with desire.

She saw me as I entered. She was glad to see me; I knew she was, because I could tell by the way her eyes widened. Her face brightened and that tight feeling caught my throat. All at once I was so happy, sure of myself, clean and conscious of my youth. I sat at that same first table. Tonight there was music in the saloon, a piano and a violin; two fat women with hard masculine faces and short haircuts. Their song was *Over the Waves*. Ta de da da, and I watched Camilla dancing with her beer tray. Her hair was so black, so deep and clustered, like grapes hiding her neck. This was a sacred place, this saloon. Everything here was holy, the chairs, the tables, that rag in her hand, that sawdust under her feet. She was a Mayan princess and this was her castle. I watched the tattered huaraches glide across the floor, and I wanted those huaraches. I would like them to hold in my hands against my chest when I fell asleep. I would like to hold them and breathe the odor of them.

She did not venture near my table, but I was glad. Don't come right away, Camilla; let me sit here awhile and accustom myself to this rare excitement; leave me alone while my mind travels the infinite loveliness of your splendid glory; just leave awhile to myself, to hunger and dream with eyes awake.

She came finally, carrying a cup of coffee in her tray. The same coffee, the same chipped, brownish mug. She came with her eyes blacker and wider than ever, walking toward me on soft feet, smiling mysteriously, until I thought I would faint from the pounding of

41

my heart. As she stood beside me, I sensed the slight odor of her perspiration mingled with the tart cleanliness of her starched smock. It overwhelmed me, made me stupid, and I breathed through my lips to avoid it. She smiled to let me know she did not object to the spilled coffee of the other evening; more than that, I seemed to feel she had rather liked the whole thing, she was glad about it, grateful for it.

"I didn't know you had freckles," she said.

"They don't mean anything," I said.

"I'm sorry about the coffee," she said. "Everybody orders beer. We don't get many calls for coffee."

"That's exactly why you don't get many calls for it. Because it's so lousy. I'd drink beer too, if I could afford it."

She pointed at my hand with a pencil. "You bite your fingernails," she said. "You shouldn't do that."

I shoved my hands in my pockets.

"Who are you to tell me what to do?"

"Do you want some beer?" she said. "I'll get you some. You don't have to pay for it."

"You don't have to get me anything. I'll drink this alleged coffee and get out of here."

She walked to the bar and ordered a beer. I watched her pay for it from a handful of coins she dug out of her smock. She carried the beer to me and placed it under my nose. It hurt me.

"Take it away," I said. "Get it out of here. I want coffee, not beer."

Someone in the rear called her name and she hurried away. The backs of her knees appeared as she bent over the table and gathered empty beer mugs. I moved in my chair, my feet kicking something under the table. It was a spittoon. She was at the bar again, nodding at me, smiling, making a motion indicating I should drink the beer. I felt devilish, vicious I got her attention and poured the beer into the spittoon. Her white teeth took hold of her lower lip and her face lost blood. Her eyes blazed. A pleasantness pervaded me, a satisfaction. I sat back and smiled to the ceiling.

She disappeared behind a thin partition which served as a

kitchen. She reappeared, smiling. Her hands were behind her back, concealing something. Now the old man I had seen that morning stepped from behind the partition. He grinned expectantly. Camilla waved to me. The worst was about to happen: I could feel it coming. From behind her back she revealed the little magazine containing *The Little Dog Laughed.* She waved it in the air, but she was out of view, and her performance was only for the old man and myself. He watched with big eyes. My mouth went dry as I saw her wet fingers and flip the pages to the place where the story was printed. Her lips twisted as she clamped the magazine between her knees and ripped away the pages. She held them over her head, waving them and smiling. The old man shook his head approvingly. The smile on her face changed to determination as she tore the pages into little pieces, and these into smaller pieces. With a gesture of finality, she let the pieces fall through her fingers and trickle to the spittoon at her feet. I tried to smile. She slapped her hands together with an air of boredom, like one slapping the dust from her palms. Then she put one hand on her hip, tilted her shoulder, and swaggered away. The old man stood there for some time. Only he had seen her. Now that the show was over, he disappeared behind the partition.

I sat smiling wretchedly, my heart weeping for *The Little Dog Laughed,* for every well-turned phrase, for the little flecks of poetry through it, my first story, the best thing I could show for my whole life. It was the record of all that was good in me, approved and printed by the great J. C. Hackmuth, and she had torn it up and thrown it into a spittoon.

After a while I pushed back my chair and got up to leave. Standing at the bar, she watched me go. There was pity for me upon her face, a tiny smile of regret for what she had done, but I kept my eyes away from her and walked into the street, glad for the hideous din of street cars and the queer noises of the city pounding my ears and burying me in an avalanche of banging and screeching. I put my hands in my pockets and slumped away.

Fifty feet from the saloon I heard someone calling. I turned around. It was she, running on soft feet, coins jingling in her pockets.

"Young fellow!" she called. "Oh kid!"

I waited and she came out of breath, speaking quickly and softly. "I'm sorry, she said. "I didn't mean anything—honest."

"It's okay," I said. "I didn't mind."

She kept glancing toward the saloon. "I have to get back," she said. "They'll miss me. Come back tomorrow night, will you? Please! I can be nice. I'm awfully sorry about tonight. Please come, please!" She squeezed my arm. "Will you come?"

"Maybe."

She smiled. "Forgive me?"

"Sure."

I stood in the middle of the sidewalk and watched her hurry back. After a few steps she turned, blew a kiss and called, "Tomorrow night. Don't forget!"

"Camilla!" I said. "Wait. Just a minute!"

We ran toward each other, meeting halfway.

"Hurry!" she said. "They'll fire me."

I glanced at her feet. She sensed it coming and I felt her recoiling from me. Now a good feeling rushed through me, a coolness, a newness like new skin. I spoke slowly.

"Those huaraches—do you have to wear them, Camilla? Do you have to emphasize the fact that you always were and always will be a filthy little Greaser?"

She looked at me in horror, her lips open. Clasping both hands against her mouth, she rushed inside the saloon. I heard her moaning. "Oh, oh, oh."

I tossed my shoulders and swaggered away, whistling with pleasure. In the gutter I saw a long cigaret butt. I picked it up without shame, lit it as I stood with one foot in the gutter, puffed it and exhaled toward the stars. I was an American, and goddamn proud of it. This great city, these mighty pavements and proud buildings, they were the voice of my America. From sand and cactus we Americans had carved an empire. Camilla's people had had their chance. They had failed. We Americans had turned the trick. Thank God for my country. Thank God I had been born an American!

Chapter Six

I went up to my room, up the dusty stairs of Bunker Hill, past the soot-covered frame buildings along that dark street, sand and oil and grease choking the futile palm trees standing like dying prisoners, chained to a little plot of ground with black pavement hiding their feet. Dust and old buildings and old people sitting at windows, old people tottering out of doors, old people moving painfully along the dark street. The old folk from Indiana and Iowa and Illinois, from Boston and Kansas City and Des Moines, they sold their homes and their stores, and they came here by train and by automobile to the land of sunshine, to die in the sun, with just enough money to live until the sun killed them, tore themselves out by the roots in their last days, deserted the smug prosperity of Kansas City and Chicago and Peoria to find a place in the sun. And when they got here they found that other and greater thieves had already taken possession, that even the sun belonged to the others; Smith and Jones and Parker, druggist, banker, baker, dust of Chicago and Cincinnati and Cleveland on their shoes, doomed to die in the sun, a few dollars in the bank, enough to subscribe to the *Los Angeles Times*, enough to keep alive the illusion that this was paradise, that their little papier-mâché homes were castles. The uprooted ones, the empty sad folks, the old and the young folks, the folks from back home. These were my countrymen, these were the new Californians. With their bright polo shirts and sunglasses, they were in paradise, they belonged.

But down on Main Street, down on Towne and San Pedro, and for a mile on lower Fifth Street were the tens of thousands of others; they couldn't afford sunglasses or a four-bit polo shirt and they hid in the alleys by day and slunk off to flop houses by night. A cop won't pick you up for vagrancy in Los Angeles if you wear a fancy polo shirt and a pair of sunglasses. But if there is dust on your shoes and that sweater you wear is thick like the sweaters they wear in the snow countries, he'll grab you. So get yourselves a polo shirt boys, and a pair of sunglasses, and white shoes, if you can. Be collegiate. It'll get you anyway. After a while, after big doses of the *Times* and the *Examiner*, you too will whoop it up for the sunny south. You'll eat hamburgers year after year and live in dusty, vermin-infested apartments and hotels, but every morning you'll see the mighty sun, the eternal blue of the sky, and the streets will be full of sleek women you never will possess, and the hot semi-tropical nights will reek of romance you'll never have, but you'll still be in paradise, boys, in the land of sunshine.

As for the folks back home, you can lie to them, because they hate the truth anyway, they won't have it, because soon or late they want to come out to paradise, too. You can't fool the folks back home, boys. They know what Southern California's like. After all they read the papers, they look at the picture magazine glutting the newsstands of every corner in America. They've seen pictures of the movie stars' homes. You can't tell them anything about California.

Lying in my bed I thought about them, watched the blobs of red light from the St. Paul Hotel jump in and out of my room, and I was miserable, for tonight I had acted like them. Smith and Parker and Jones, I had never been one of them. Ah, Camilla! When I was a kid back home in Colorado it was Smith and Parker and Jones who hurt me with their hideous names, called me Wop and Dago and Greaser, and their children hurt me, just as I hurt you tonight. They hurt me so much I could never become one of them, drove me to books, drove me within myself, drove me to run away from that Colorado town, and sometimes, Camilla, when I see their faces I feel the hurt all over again, the old ache there, and sometimes I am glad they are here, dying in the sun, uprooted, tricked by their heartlessness, the same faces, the same set, hard mouths, faces from my home town, fulfilling the emptiness of their lives under a blazing sun.

I see them in the lobbies of hotels, I see them sunning in the parks, and limping out of ugly little churches, their faces bleak from proximity with their strange gods, out of Aimee's Temple, out of the Church of the Great I Am.

I have seen them stagger out of their movie palaces and blink their empty eyes in the face of reality once more, and stagger home, to read the *Times*, to find out what's going on in the world. I have vomited at their newspapers, read their literature, observed their customs, eaten their food, desired their women, gaped at their art. But I am poor, and my name ends with a soft vowel, and they hate me and my father, and my father's father, and they would have my blood and put me down, but they are old now, dying in the sun and in the hot dust of the road, and I am young and full of hope and love for my country and my times, and when I say Greaser to you it is not my heart that speaks, but the quivering of an old wound, and I am ashamed of the terrible thing I have done.

Chapter Seven

I am thinking of the Alta Loma Hotel, remembering the people who lived there. I remember my first day there. I remember that I walked into the dark lobby carrying two suitcases, one of them filled with copies of *The Little Dog Laughed*. It was a long time ago, but I remember it well. I had come by bus, dusty to the skin, the dust of Wyoming and Utah and Nevada in my hair and in my ears.

"I want a cheap room," I said.

The landlady had white hair. Around her neck was a high net collar fitting tightly like a corset. She was in her seventies, a tall woman who increased her height by rising on tiptoe and peering at me over her glasses.

"Do you have a job?" she said.

"I'm a writer," I said. "Look, I'll show you."

I opened my suitcase and got out a copy. "I wrote that," I told her. I was eager in those days, very proud. "I'll give you a copy," I said. "I'll autograph it for you."

I took a fountain pen from the desk, it was dry and I had to dip it, and I rolled my tongue around thinking of something nice to say. "What's your name?" I asked her. She told me unwillingly. "Mrs. Hargraves," she said. "Why?" But I was honoring her, and I had no time to answer questions, and I wrote above the story, "For a woman of ineffable charm, with lovely blue eyes and a generous smile, from the author, Arturo Bandini."

She smiled with a smile that seemed to hurt her face, cracking it open with old lines that broke up the dry flesh around her mouth and cheeks. "I hate dog stories," she said, putting the magazine out of sight. She looked at me from an even higher view over her glasses. "Young man," she said, "are you a Mexican?"

I pointed at myself and laughed.

"Me, a Mexican?" I shook my head. "I'm an American, Mrs. Hargraves. And that isn't a dog story, either. It's about a man, it's pretty good. There isn't a dog in the whole story."

"We don't allow Mexicans in this hotel," she said.

"I'm not a Mexican. I got that title after the fable. You know: 'And the little dog laughed to see such sport.'"

"Nor Jews," she said.

I registered. I had a beautiful signature in those days, intricate, oriental, illegible, with a mighty slashing underscore, a signature more complex than that of the great Hackmuth. And after the signature I wrote, "Boulder, Colorado."

She examined the script, word for word.

Coldly: "What's your name, young man?"

And I was disappointed, for already she had forgotten the author of *The Little Dog Laughed* and his name printed in large type on the magazine. I told her my name. She printed it carefully over the signature. Then she crossed the page to the other writing.

"Mr. Bandini," she said, looking at me coldly, "Boulder is *not* in Colorado."

"It is too!" I said. "I just came from there. It was there two days ago."

She was firm, determined. "Boulder is in Nebraska. My husband and I went through Boulder, Nebraska, thirty years ago, on our way out here. You will kindly change that, if you please."

"But it *is* in Colorado! My mother lives there, my father. I went to school there!"

She reached under the desk and drew out the magazine. She handed it to me. "This hotel is no place for you, young man. We have fine people here, honest people."

I didn't accept the magazine. I was so tired, hammered to bits by the long bus ride. "All right," I said. "It's in Nebraska." And I wrote it down, scratched out the Colorado and wrote Nebraska over it. She was satisfied, very pleased with me, smiled and examined the magazine. "So you're an author!" she said. "How nice!" Then she put the magazine out of sight again. "Welcome to California!" she said. "You'll love it here!"

That Mrs. Hargraves! She was lonely, and so lost and still proud. One afternoon she took me to her apartment on the top floor. It was like walking into a well-dusted tomb. Her husband was dead now, but thirty years ago he had owned a tool shop in Bridgeport, Connecticut. His picture was on the wall. A splendid man, who neither smoked nor drank, dead of a heart attack; a thin, severe face out of a heavy framed picture, still contemptuous of smoking and drinking. Here was the bed in which he died, a high mahogany four-poster; here were his clothes in the closet and his shoes on the floor, the toes turned upward from age. Here on the mantel was his shaving mug, he always shaved himself, and his name was Bert. That Bert! Bert, she used to say, why don't you go to the barber, and Bert would laugh, because he knew he was a better barber than the regular barbers.

Bert always got up at five in the morning. He came from a family of fifteen children. He was handy with tools. He had done all the repair work around the hotel for years. It had taken him three weeks to paint the outside of the building. He used to say he was a better painter than the regular painters. For two hours she talked of Bert, and Lord! how she loved that man, even in death, but he was not dead at all; he was in that apartment, watching over her, protecting her, daring me to hurt her. He frightened me, and made me want to rush away. We had tea. The tea was old. The sugar was old and lumpish. The tea cups were dusty, and somehow the tea tasted old and the little dried up cookies tasted of death. When I got up to leave, Bert followed me through the door and down the hall, daring me to think cynically of him. For two nights he hounded me, threatened me, even cajoled me in the matter of cigarets.

I am remembering that kid from Memphis. I never asked his name and he never asked mine. We said "Hi" to one another. He was not there long, a few weeks. His pimpled face was always covered by his long hands when he sat on the front porch of the hotel: every night late he was there; twelve and one and two o'clock, and coming home I would find him rocking back and forth in the wicker chair, his nervous fingers picking at his face, searching his uncut black hair. "Hi," I would say, and "Hi" he would answer.

The restless dust of Los Angeles fevered him. He was a greater wanderer than myself, and all day long he sought out perverse loves in the parks. But he was so ugly he never found his desire, and the warm nights with low stars and yellow moon tortured him away from his room until the dawn arrived. But one night he talked to me, left me nauseated and unhappy as he reveled in memories of Memphis, Tennessee, where the real people came from, where there were friends and friends. Some day he would leave this hated city, some day he would go back where friendship meant something, and sure enough, he went away and I got a postcard signed "Memphis Kid" from Fort Worth, Texas.

There was Heilman, who belonged to the Book of the Month Club. A huge man with arms like logs and legs tight in his pants. He was a bank teller. He had a wife in Moline, Illinois and a son at the University of Chicago. He hated the southwest, his hatred bulging from his big face, but his health was bad, and he was doomed to stay here or die. He sneered at everything western. He was sick after every intersectional football game that saw the east defeated. He spat when you mentioned the Trojans. He hated the sun, cursed the fog, denounced the rain, dreamed always of the snows of the middle-west. Once a month his letter box had a big package. I saw him in the lobby, always reading. He wouldn't lend me his books.

"A matter of principle," Heilman said.

But he gave me the *Book of the Month Club News,* a little magazine about new books. Every month he left it in my letter box.

And the redheaded girl from St. Louis who always asked about the Filipinos. Where did they live? How many were there? Did I know any of them? A gaunt redheaded girl, with brown freckles below the neckline of her dress, out here from St. Louis. She wore green all the time, her copper head too startling for beauty, her eyes too grey for her face. She got a job in a laundry, but the pay was too little, so she quit. She too wandered the warm streets. Once she lent me a quarter, another time, postage stamps. End-

51

lessly she spoke of the Filipinos, pitied them, thought them so brave in the face of prejudice. One day she was gone, and another day I saw her again, walking the streets, her copper hair catching sunbeams, a short Filipino holding her arm. He was very proud of her. His padded shoulders and tight waisted suit were the ultimate of tenderloin fashion, but even with the high leather heels he was a foot shorter than she.

Of them all, only one read *The Little Dog Laughed.* Those first days I autographed a great number of copies, brought them upstairs to the waiting room. Five or six copies, and I placed them conspicuously everywhere, on the library table, on the divan, even in the deep leather chairs so that to sit down you had to pick them up. Nobody read them, not a soul, except one. For a week they were spread about, but they were hardly touched. Even when the Japanese boy dusted that room he never so much as lifted them from where they lay. In the evenings people played bridge in there, and a group of the old guests gathered to talk and relax. I slipped in, found a chair, and watched. It was disheartening. A big woman in one of the deep chairs had even seated herself upon a copy, not bothering to remove it. A day came when the Japanese boy piled the copies neatly together on the library table. They gathered dust. Once in awhile, every few days, I rubbed my handkerchief over them and scattered them about. They always returned untouched to the neat stack on the library table. Maybe they knew I had written it, and deliberately avoided it. Maybe they simply didn't care. Not even Heilman, with all his reading. Not even the landlady. I shook my head: they were very foolish, all of them. It was a story about their own middle-west, about Colorado and a snowstorm, and there they were with their uprooted souls and sun-burned faces, dying in a blazing desert, and the cool homelands from whence they came were so near at hand, right there in the pages of that little magazine. And I thought, ah well, it was ever thus—Poe, Whitman, Heine, Dreiser, and now Bandini; thinking that, I was not so hurt, not so lonely.

The name of the person who read my story was Judy, and her last name was Palmer. She knocked on my door that afternoon, and opening it, I saw her. She was holding a copy of the magazine in her hand. She was only fourteen, with bangs of brown hair, and a red ribbon tied in a bow above her forehead.

"Are you Mr. Bandini?" she said.

I could tell from her eyes she had read *The Little Dog Laughed.* I could tell instantly. "You read my story, didn't you?" I said. "How did you like it?"

She clutched it close to her chest and smiled. "I think it's wonderful," she said. "Oh, so wonderful! Mrs. Hargraves told me you wrote it. She told me you might give me a copy."

My heart fluttered in my throat.

"Come in!" I said. "Welcome! Have a chair! What's your name? Of course you can have a copy. Of course! But please come in!"

I ran across the room and got her the best chair. She sat down so delicately, the child's dress she wore not even concealing her knees. "Do you want a glass of water?" I said. "It's a hot day. Maybe you're thirsty."

But she wasn't. She was only nervous. I could see I frightened her. I tried to be nicer, for I didn't want to scare her away. It was in those early days when I still had a bit of money. "Do you like ice cream?" I said. "Would you like me to get you a milk nickel or something?"

"I can't stay," she said. "Mother will get angry."

"Do you live here?" I said. "Did your mother read the story too? What's your name?" I smiled proudly. "Of course you already know my name," I said. "I'm Arturo Bandini."

"Oh, yes!" she breathed, and her eyes widened with such admiration I wanted to throw myself at her feet and weep. I could feel it in my throat, the ticklish impulse to start sobbing.

"Are you sure you won't have some ice cream?"

She had such beautiful manners, sitting there with her pink chin tilted, her tiny hands clinging to the magazine. "No thank you, Mr. Bandini."

"How about a Coke?" I said.

"Thank you," she smiled. "No."

"Root beer?"

"No, if you please. Thank you."

"What's your name?" I said. "Mine's—" but I stopped in time.

"Judy," she said.

"Judy!" I said, over and over. "Judy, Judy! It's wonderful!" I said. "It's like the name of a star. It's the most beautiful name I ever heard!"

"Thank you!" she said.

I opened the dresser drawer containing copies of my story. It was still wellstocked, some fifteen remaining. "I'm going to give you a clean copy," I told her. "And I'm going to autograph it. Something nice, something extra special!"

Her face colored with delight. This little girl was not joking; she was really thrilled, and her joy was like cool water running down my face. "I'm going to give you two copies," I said. "And I'm going to autograph both of them!"

"You're such a nice man," she said. She was studying me as I opened an ink bottle. "I could tell by your story."

"I'm not a man," I said. "I'm not much older than you, Judy." I didn't want to be old before her. I wanted to cut it down as much as possible. "I'm only eighteen," I lied.

"Is that all?" she was astonished.

"Be nineteen in a couple of months."

I wrote something special in both the magazines. I don't remember the words but it was good, what I wrote, it came from my heart because I was so grateful. But I wanted more, to hear her voice that was so small and breathless, to keep her there in my room as long as I could.

"You would do me a great honor," I said. "You would make me terribly happy, Judy, if you'd read my story out loud to me. It's never happened, and I'd like to hear it."

"I'd love to read it!" she said, and she sat erect, rigid with eagerness. I threw myself on the bed, buried my face in the pillow, and the little girl read my story with a soft sweet voice that had me weeping at the first hundred words. It was like a dream, the voice of an angel filling the room, and in a little while she was sobbing too, interrupting her reading now and then with gulps and chokes, and protesting. "I can't read anymore," she would say, "I can't." And I would turn over and beseech her: "But you've got to, Judy. Oh, you got to!"

As we reached the high point of our emotion, a tall, bitter-mouthed woman suddenly entered the room without knocking. I knew it was Judy's mother. Her fierce eyes studied me, and then Judy. Without a word she took Judy's hand and led her away. The little girl clutched the magazines to her thin breast, and over her shoulder she blinked a tearful goodbye. She had come and gone as quickly as that, and I never saw her again. It was a mystery to the landlady too, for they had arrived and departed that very day, not even staying over night.

Chapter Eight

There was a letter from Hackmuth in my box. I knew it was from Hackmuth. I could tell a Hackmuth letter a mile away. I could feel a Hackmuth letter, and it felt like an icicle sliding down my spine. Mrs. Hargraves handed the letter to me. I grabbed it out of her hand.

"Good news?" she said, because I owed her so much rent. "You never can tell," I said. "But it's from a great man. He could send blank pages, and it would be good news to me."

But I knew it wasn't good news in the sense that Mrs. Hargraves meant it, for I hadn't sent mighty Hackmuth a story. This was merely the answer to my long letter of a few days ago. He was very prompt, that Hackmuth. He dazzled you with his speed. You no sooner dropped a letter in the mail box down on the corner, and when you got back to the hotel, there was his answer. Ah me, but his letters were so brief. A forty page letter, and he replied in one small paragraph. But that was fine in its way, because his replies were easier to memorize and know by heart. He had a way, that Hackmuth; he had a style; he had so much to give, even his commas and semi-colons had a way of dancing up and down. I used to tear the stamps off his envelopes, peel them off gently, to see what was under them.

I sat on the bed and opened the letter. It was another brief message, no more than fifty words. It said:

Dear Mr. Bandini,
With your permission I shall remove the salutation and
ending of your long letter and print it as a short story for
my magazine. It seems to me you have done a fine job
here. I think "The Long Lost Hills" would serve as an

excellent title. My check is enclosed.
                    Sincerely yours,
                    J. C. Hackmuth.

The letter slipped from my fingers and zigzagged to the floor. I stood up and looked in the mirror. My mouth was wide open. I walked to Hackmuth's picture on the opposite wall and put my fingers on the firm face that looked out at me. I picked the letter up and read it again. I opened the window, climbed out, and lay in the bright hillside grass. My fingers clawed the grass. I rolled upon my stomach, sank my mouth into the earth, and pulled the grass roots with my teeth. Then I started to cry. Oh God, Hackmuth! How can you be such a wonderful man? How is it possible? I climbed back to my room and found the check inside the envelope. It was $175. I was a rich man once more. $175! Arturo Bandini, author of *The Little Dog Laughed* and *The Long Lost Hills*.

I stood before the mirror once more, shaking my fist defiantly. Here I am, folks. Take a look at a great writer! Notice my eyes, folks. The eyes of a great writer. Notice my jaw, folks. The jaw of a great writer. Look at those hands, folks. The hands that created *The Little Dog Laughed* and *The Long Lost Hills*. I pointed my index finger savagely. And as for you, Camilla Lopez, I want to see you tonight. I want to talk to you, Camilla Lopez. And I warn you, Camilla Lopez, remember that you stand before none other than Arturo Bandini, the writer. Remember that, if you please.

Mrs. Hargraves cashed the check. I paid my back rent and two months' rent in advance. She wrote out a receipt for the full amount. I waved it aside. "Please," I said. "Don't bother, Mrs. Hargraves. I trust you completely." She insisted. I put the receipt in my pocket. Then I laid an extra five dollars on the desk. "For you, Mrs. Hargraves. Because you've been so nice." She refused it. She pushed it back. "Ridiculous!" she said. But I wouldn't take it. I walked out and she hurried after me, chased me into the street.

"Mr. Bandini, I insist you take this money."

Pooh, a mere five dollars, a trifle. I shook my head. "Mrs. Hargraves, I absolutely refuse to take it." We haggled, stood in the middle of the sidewalk under the hot sun and argued. She was adamant. She begged me to take it back. I smiled quietly. "No, Mrs. Hargraves, I'm sorry. I never change my mind."

She walked away, pale with anger, holding the five dollar bill between her fingers as though she were carrying a dead mouse. I shook my head. Five dollars! A pittance as far as Arturo Bandini, author of numerous stories for J. C. Hackmuth, was concerned.

I walked downtown, fought my way through the hot cramped streets to The May Company basement. It was the finest suit of clothes I ever bought, a brown pin-stripe with two pairs of pants. Now I could be well dressed at all times. I bought two-tone brown and white shoes, a lot of shirts and a lot of socks, and a hat. My first hat, dark brown, real felt with a white silk lining. The pants had to be altered. I told them to hurry. It was done in a little while. I changed behind a curtain stall, put on everything new, with the hat to top it off. The clerk wrapped my old clothes in a box. I didn't want them. I told him to call up the Salvation Army, to give them away, and to deliver the other purchases to my hotel. On the way out I bought a pair of sunglasses. I spent the rest of the afternoon buying things, killing time. I bought cigarets, candy and candied fruit. I bought two reams of expensive paper, rubber bands, paper clips, note pads, a small filing cabinet, and a gadget for punching holes in paper. I also bought a cheap watch, a bed lamp, a comb, toothbrushes, tooth paste, hair lotion, shaving cream, skin lotion, and a first aid kit. I stopped at a tie shop and bought ties, a new belt, a watch chain, handkerchiefs, bathrobe and bedroom slippers. Evening came, and I couldn't carry any more. I called a taxi and rode home.

I was very tired. Sweat soaked through my new suit, and crawled down my leg to my ankles. But this was fun. I took a bath, rubbed the lotion into my skin, and washed my teeth with the new brush and paste. Then I shaved with the new cream and doused my hair with the lotion. For a while I sat around in my bedroom slippers and bathrobe, put away my new paper and gadgets, smoked good, fresh cigarets and ate candy.

The deliveryman from The May Company brought the rest of my purchases in a big box. I opened it and found not only the new stuff but also my old clothes. These I tossed into the wastebasket. Now it was time to dress again. I got into a pair of new shorts, a brand new shirt, socks, and the other pair of pants. Then I put on a tie and my new shoes. Standing at the mirror, I tilted my hat over on eye, and examined myself. The image in the glass seemed only vaguely familiar. I didn't like my new tie, so I took off my coat and tried another. I didn't like the change either. All at once everything began to irritate me. The stiff collar was strangling me. The shoes pinched my feet. The pants smelled like a clothing store basement and were too tight in the crotch. Sweat broke out at my temples where the hat band squeezed my skull. Suddenly I began to itch, and when I moved everything crackled like a paper sack. My nostrils picked up the powerful stench of lotions, and I grimaced. Mother in Heaven, what had happened to the old Bandini, author of *The Little Dog Laughed?* Could this hog-tied, strangling buffoon be the creator of *The Long Lost Hills?* I pulled everything off, washed the smells out of my hair, and climbed into my old clothes. They were very glad to have me again; they clung to me with cool delight, and my tormented feet slipped into the old shoes as into the softness of Spring grass.

Chapter Nine

I rode down to the Columbia Buffet in a taxi. The driver wheeled to the curb directly in front of the open door. I got out and handed him a twenty dollar bill. He didn't have the change. I was glad because when I finally found a smaller bill and paid him off, there was Camilla standing in the door. Very few taxis stopped before the Columbia Buffet. I nodded casually to Camilla and walked in and sat at the first table. I was reading Hackmuth's letter when she spoke.

"Are you mad at me?" she said.

"Not that I know of," I said.

She put her hands behind her and looked down at her feet. "Don't I look different?"

She was wearing new white pumps, with high heels.

"They're very nice," I said, turning to Hackmuth's letter once more. She watched me with a pout. I glanced up and winked. "Excuse me," I said. "Business."

"You want to order anything?"

"A cigar," I said. "Something expensive from Havana."

She brought the box. I took one.

"They're expensive," she said. "A quarter."

I smiled and gave her a dollar.

"Keep the change."

She refused the tip.

"Not from you," she said. "You're poor."

"I used to be," I said. I lit the cigar, let the smoke tumble out of my mouth as I leaned far back and stared at the ceiling. "Not a bad cigar for the money," I said.

The female musicians in the rear were hacking out *Over the Waves*. I made a face and pushed the change from the cigar toward

Camilla. "Tell them to play Strauss," I said. "Something Viennese."

She picked up a quarter, but I made her take it all. The musicians were aghast. Camilla pointed at me. They waved and beamed. I nodded with dignity. They plunged into *Tales from the Vienna Woods*. The new shoes were hurting Camilla's feet. She didn't have her old sparkle. She winced as she walked, gritted her teeth.

"You want a beer?" she asked.

"I want a Scotch highball," I said. "St. James."

She discussed it with the bartender, then came back. "We don't have St. James. We have Ballantine's, though. It's expensive. Forty cents."

I ordered one for myself and one each for the two bartenders. "You shouldn't spend your money like that," she said. I acknowledged the toast from the two bartenders, and then I sipped my highball. I screwed up my face.

"Rotgut," I said.

She stood with her hands stuffed inside her pockets.

"I thought you'd like my new shoes," she said.

I had resumed the reading of Hackmuth's letter.

"They seem all right," I said.

She limped away to a table just vacated and began picking up empty beer mugs. She was hurt, her face long and sad. I sipped the highball and went on reading and rereading Hackmuth's letter. In a little while she returned to my table.

"You've changed," she said. "You're different. I liked you better the other way."

I smiled and patted her hand. It was warm, sleek, brown, with long fingers. "Little Mexican princess," I said. "You're so charming, so innocent."

She jerked her hand away and her face lost color.

"I'm *not* a Mexican!" she said. "I'm an American."

I shook my head.

"No," I said. "To me you'll always be a sweet little peon. A flower girl from old Mexico."

"You dago sonofabitch!" she said.

It blinded me, but I went on smiling. She stomped away, the shoes hurting her, restraining her angry legs. I was sick inside, and my smile felt as though tacks held it there. She was at a table near the musicians, wiping it off, her arm churning furiously, her face like a dark flame. When she looked at me the hatred out of her eyes bolted across the room. Hackmuth's letter no longer interested me. I stuffed it into my pocket and sat with my head down. It was an old feeling, and I traced it back and remembered that it was a feeling I had the first time I sat in the place. She disappeared behind the partition. When she returned she moved gracefully, her feet quick and sure. She had taken off the white shoes and put on the old huaraches.

"I'm sorry," she said.

"No," I said. "It's my fault, Camilla."

"I didn't mean what I said."

"You were alright. It was my fault."

I looked down at her feet.

"Those white shoes were so beautiful. You have such lovely legs and they fitted so perfectly."

She put her fingers through my hair, and the warmth of her pleasure poured through them, and through me, and my throat was hot, and a deep happiness seeped through my flesh. She went behind the partition and emerged wearing the white shoes. The little muscles in her jaws contracted as she walked, but she smiled bravely. I watched her at work, and the sight of her lifted me, a buoyancy like oil upon water. After a while she asked me if I had a car. I told her I didn't. She said she had one, it was in the parking lot next door, and she described her car, and we arranged to meet in the parking lot and then drive out to the beach. As I got up to leave the tall bartender with the white face looked at me with what seemed the faintest trace of a leer. I walked out, ignoring it.

Her car was a 1929 Ford roadster with horsehair bursting from upholstery, battered fenders and no top. I sat in it and fooled with the gadgets. I looked at the owner's certificate. It was made out to Camilla Lombard, not Camilla Lopez.

She was with somebody when she entered the lot, but I couldn't see who it was because it was so dark, no moonlight and a thin web of fog. Then they came closer, and it was the tall bartender. She introduced him, his name was Sammy, and he was quiet and not interested. We drove him home, down Spring Street to First and over the railroad tracks to a black neighborhood that picked up the sounds of the rattling Ford and threw the echoes over an area of dirty frame houses and tired picket fences. He got out at a place where a dying pepper tree had spilled its brown leaves over the ground, and when he walked to the porch you could hear his feet wading through the hissing dead leaves.

"Who is he?" I said.

He was just a friend, she said, and she didn't want to talk about him, but she was worried about him; her face assumed that solicitous cast one gets from concern over a sick friend. This worried me, made me jealous all at once, and I kept after her with little questions, and the drawling way she answered made it worse. We went back over the tracks and through the downtown section. She would go right through a stop signal if no cars were around, and when anyone got in her way she would smash her palm on the squealing horn and hold it there. The sound rose like a cry of help through the canyons of buildings. She kept doing this, no matter whether she needed it or not. I cautioned her once, but she ignored it.

"I'm driving this car," she said.

We got to Wilshire where the traffic was regulated to a minimum of thirty-five. The Ford couldn't travel that fast, but she clung to the middle lane and big fast cars shot around us. They infuriated her and she shook her fist and cursed them. After a mile she complained about her feet and asked me to hold the wheel. As I did it she reached down and took off her shoes. Then she took the wheel again and threw one foot over the side of the Ford. At once her dress ballooned out, spanked her face. She tucked it under herself, but even so her brown thighs were exposed even to a pinkish underthing. It drew a lot of attention. Motorists shot by, pulled up short, and heads came out of windows to observe her brown naked leg. It made her angry. She took to shouting at the spectators,

63

yelling that they ought to mind their own business. I sat at her side, slouched down, trying to enjoy a cigaret that burned too hotly in the rush of wind.

Then we got to a major stop-signal at Western and Wilshire. It was a busy corner, a movie palace and night clubs and drug stores pouring pedestrians into the street. She couldn't go through that signal because so many other cars were in front of us, waiting the change of light. She sat back, impatient, nervous, swinging her leg. Faces began to turn our way, horns tooted gaily, and behind us a fancy roadster with an impish klaxon sent out an insistent yoohoo. She turned around, her eyes ablaze, and shook her fist at the collegians in the roadster. By now every eye was on us, and everyone smiled. I nudged her.

"Pull it in at stop signals, at least."

"Oh shut up!" she said.

I reached for Hackmuth's letter and sought refuge in it. The boulevard was well-lighted, I could read the words, but the Ford kicked like a mule, rattled and jerked and broke wind. She was proud of that car.

"It's got a wonderful engine," she said.

"It sounds good," I said, hanging on.

"You ought to have a car of your own," she said.

I asked her about the Camilla Lombard written on her owner's certificate. I asked her if she was married.

"No," she said.

"What's the Lombard for?"

"For fun," she said. "Sometimes I use it professionally."

I didn't understand.

"Do you like your name?" she asked. "Don't you wish it was Johnson, or Williams, or something?"

I said no, that I was satisfied.

"No you're not," she said. "I know."

"But I am!" I said.

"No you're not."

After Beverly Hills there was no fog. The palms along the road stood out green in the bluish darkness, and the white line in the pavement leaped ahead of us like a burning fuse. A few clouds tumbled and tossed, but there were no stars. We passed through low hills. On both sides of the road were high hedges and lush vines with wild palms and cypress trees scattered everywhere.

In silence we reached the Palisades, driving along the crest of the high cliffs overlooking the sea. A cold wind sideswiped us. The jalopy teetered. From below rose the roar of the sea. Far out fog-banks crept toward the land, an army of ghosts crawling on their bellies. Below us the breakers flayed the land with white fists. They retreated and came back to flay it again. As each breaker retreated, the shoreline broke into an ever-widening grin. We coasted in second down the spiral road, the black pavement perspiring, fog tongues licking it. The air was so clean. We breathed it gratefully. There was no dust here.

She drove the car into an endless stretch of white sand. We sat and watched the sea. It was warm below the cliffs. She touched my hand. "Why don't you teach me to swim?" she said.

"Not out there," I said.

The breakers were tall. The tide was high and they came in fast. A hundred yards out they formed and came in all the way. We watched them burst against the shore, foamy lace exploding like thunder.

"You learn to swim in still water," I said.

She laughed and began undressing. She was brown underneath, but it was natural brown and not a tan. I was white and ghostlike. There was a blob of heaviness at my stomach. I pulled it in to hide it. She looked at the whiteness, at my loins and legs, and smiled. I was glad when she walked toward the water.

The sand was soft and warm. We sat facing the sea and talked of swimming. I showed her the first principles. She lay on her stomach, paddled her hands and kicked her feet. Sand sprinkled her face and she imitated me without enthusiasm. She sat up.

"I don't like learning to swim," she said.

We waded hand in hand into the water, our fronts caked with sand. It was cold, then just right. It was my first time in the ocean. I breasted the waves until my shoulders were under water, then I tried to swim. The waves lifted me. I began diving under oncoming breakers. They poured over me harmlessly. I was learning. When the big breakers appeared, I threw myself at their crests and they coasted me to the beach.

I kept my eye on Camilla. She waded to her knees, saw a breaker coming, and ran toward the shore. Then she came back. She shouted with delight. A breaker struck her and she squealed and disappeared. A moment later she reappeared, laughing and shouting. I yelled at her not to take such chances, but she staggered out to meet a white crest that rose up and tumbled her out of sight. I watched her roll like a hamper of bananas. She waded to the shore, her body glistening, her hands in her hair. I swam until I was tired, then I waded out of the water. My eyes stung from salt water. I lay on my back and panted. After a few minutes my strength returned and I sat up and felt like smoking a cigaret. Camilla was not in sight. I walked to the car, thinking she was there. But she wasn't. I ran down to the edge of the water and searched the foamy confusion. I called her name.

Then I heard her scream. It came from far out, beyond the surge of breakers and into the fog bank over choppy water. It seemed a good hundred yards. She screamed again: "Help!" I waded in, hit the first breakers with my shoulders, and started swimming. Then I lost the sound of her voice in the roar. "I'm coming!" I yelled, and I yelled it again and again, until I had to stop to save my strength. The big breakers were easy, I dived under them, but the small waves confused me, slapped my face and choked me. Finally I was in choppy water. The little waves leaped for my mouth. Her cries had stopped. I churned water with my hands, waiting for another cry. It did not come. I shouted. My voice was weak, like a voice under water.

Suddenly I was exhausted. The little waves leaped over me. I swallowed water, I was sinking. I prayed, I groaned and fought the water, and I knew I should not fight it. The sea was quiet out here. Far inland I heard the roar of the breakers. I called, waited, called again. No answer save the slush of my arms and the sound of the little choppy waves. Then something happened to my right leg, to the toes of the foot. They seemed lodged. When I kicked the pain shot to the thigh. I wanted to live. God, don't take me now! I swam blindly toward the shore.

Then I felt myself in the big breakers once more, heard them booming louder. It seemed too late. I couldn't swim, my arms were so tired, my right leg ached so much. To breathe was all that mattered. Under water the current rushed, rolling and dragging me. So this was the end of Camilla, and this was the end of Arturo Bandini—but even then I was writing it all down, seeing it across a page in a typewriter, writing it out and coasting along the sharp sand, so sure I would never come out alive. Then I was in water to my waist, limp and too far gone to do anything about it, floundering helplessly with my mind clear, composing the whole thing, worrying about excessive adjectives. The next breaker smashed me under once more, dragged me to water a foot deep, and I crawled on my hands and knees out of water a foot deep, wondering if I could perhaps make a poem out of it. I thought of Camilla out there and I sobbed and noticed that my tears were saltier than the sea water. But I couldn't lie there, I had to get help somewhere, and I got to my feet and staggered toward the car. I was so cold and my jaws chattered.

I turned and looked at the sea. Not fifty feet away Camilla waded toward the land in water to her waist. She was laughing, choking from it, this supreme joke she had played, and when I saw her dive ahead of the next breaker with all the grace and perfection of a seal, I didn't think it was funny at all. I walked out to her, felt my strength returning with every step, and when I got to her I picked her up bodily, over my shoulders, and I didn't mind her screaming, her fingers scratching my scalp and tearing my hair. I lifted her as high as my arms and threw her in a pool of water a few feet deep. She landed with a thud that knocked the breath out of her. I waded out, took her hair in both my hands, and rubbed her face and mouth in the muddy sand. I left her there, crawling on her hands and knees, crying and moaning, and I walked back to the car. She had mentioned blankets in the rumble seat. I pulled them out, wrapped myself up, and lay down on the warm sand.

In a little while she made her way through the deep sand and found me sitting under the blankets. Dripping and clean she stood before me, showing herself, proud of her nakedness, turning round and round.

"You still like me?"

I stole glances at her. I was speechless, and I nodded and grinned. She stepped upon the blankets and asked me to move over. I made a place and she slipped under, her body sleek and cold. She asked me to hold her, and I held her, and she kissed me, her lips wet and cool. We lay a long time, and I was worried and afraid and without passion. Something like a grey flower grew between us, a thought that took shape and spoke of the chasm that separated us. I didn't know what it was. I felt her waiting. I drew my hands over her belly and legs, felt my own desire, searched foolishly for my passion, strained for it while she waited, rolled and tore my hair and begged for it, but there was none, there was none at all, only the retreat to Hackmuth's letter and thoughts that remained to be written, but no lust, only fear of her, and shame and humiliation. Then I was blaming and cursing myself and I wanted to get up and walk into the sea. She felt my retreat. With a sneer she sat up and began drying her hair on the blanket.

"I thought you liked me," she said.

I couldn't answer. I shrugged and stood up. We dressed and drove back to Los Angeles. We didn't speak. She lit a cigaret and looked at me strangely, her lips pursed. She blew smoke from her cigaret into my face. I took the cigaret out of her mouth and threw it into the street. She lit another and inhaled languidly, amused and contemptuous. I hated her then.

Dawn climbed the mountains in the east, gold bars of light cutting the sky like searchlights. I took out Hackmuth's letter and read it again. Back East in New York Hackmuth would just now be entering his office. Somewhere in that office was my manuscript *The Long Lost Hills*. Love wasn't everything. Women weren't everything. A writer had to conserve his energies.

We reached the city. I told her where I lived.

"Bunker Hill?" She laughed. "It's a good place for you."

"It's perfect," I said. "In my hotel they don't allow Mexicans."

It sickened both of us. She drove to the hotel and killed the engine. I sat wondering if there was anything more to say, but there was nothing. I got out, nodded, and walked toward the hotel. Between my shoulder blades I felt her eyes like knives. As I got to the door she called me. I walked back to the car.

"Aren't you going to kiss me goodnight?"

I kissed her.

"Not that way."

Her arms slipped around my neck. She pulled my face down and sank her teeth into my lower lip. It stung and I fought her until I was free. She sat with one arm over the seat, smiling and watching me enter the hotel. I took out my handkerchief and dabbed my lips. The handkerchief had a spot of blood on it. I walked down the grey hall to my room. As I closed the door all the desire that had not come a while before seized me. It pounded my skull and tingled in my fingers. I threw myself on the bed and tore the pillow with my hands.

Chapter Ten

All that day it was on my mind. I remembered her brown nakedness and her kiss, the flavor of her mouth as it came cold from the sea, and I saw myself white and virginal, pulling in the pudgy line of my stomach, standing in the sand and holding my hands over my loins. I walked up and down the room. Late in the afternoon I was exhausted and the sight of myself in the mirror was unbearable. I sat at the typewriter and wrote about it, poured it out the way it should have happened, hammered it out with such violence that the portable typewriter kept moving away from me and across the table. On paper I stalked her like a tiger and beat her to the earth and overpowered her with my invincible strength. It ended with her creeping after me in the sand, tears streaming from her eyes, beseeching me to have mercy upon her. Fine. Excellent. But when I read it over it was ugly and dull. I tore the pages and threw them away.

Hellfrick knocked on the door. He was pale and trembling, his skin like wet paper. He was off the booze; never would he touch another drop. He sat on the edge of my bed and wrung his bony fingers. Nostalgically he talked of meat, of the good old steaks you got back in Kansas City, of the wonderful T-bones and tender lamb chops. But not out here in this land of the eternal sun, where the cattle ate nothing but dead weeds and sunshine, where the meat was full of worms and they had to paint it to make it look bloody and red. And would I lend him fifty cents? I gave him the money and he went down to the butcher shop on Olive Street. In a little while he was back in his room and the lower floor of the hotel was fragrant with the tangy aroma of liver and onions. I walked into his room. He sat before a plate of the food, his mouth bloated, his thin jaws working hard. He shook his fork at me. "I'll make it good with you, kid. I'll pay you back a thousand times."

It made me hungry. I walked down to the restaurant near Angel's Flight and ordered the same thing. I took my time having dinner. But no matter how long I loitered over coffee I knew I would eventually walk down the Flight to the Columbia Buffet. I had only to touch the lump on my lip to grow angry, and then to feel passion.

When I got down to the buffet I was afraid to enter. I crossed the street and watched her through the windows. She was not wearing her white shoes, and she seemed the same, happy and busy with her beer tray.

I got an idea. I walked quickly, two blocks, to the telegraph office. I sat down before the telegraph blank, my heart pounding. The words writhed across the page. I love you Camilla I want to marry you Arturo Bandini. When I paid for it the clerk looked at the address and said it would be delivered in ten minutes. I hurried back to Spring Street and stood in the shadowed doorway waiting for the telegraph boy to appear.

The moment I saw him coming around the corner I knew the telegram was a blunder. I ran into the street and stopped him. I told him I wrote the telegram and didn't want it delivered. "A mistake," I said. He wouldn't listen. He was tall with a pimply face. I offered him ten dollars. He shook his head and smiled emphatically. Twenty dollars, thirty.

"Not for ten million," he said.

I walked back to the shadows and watched him deliver the telegram. She was amazed to get it. I saw her finger point at herself, her face dubious. Even after she signed for it she stood holding it in her hand, watching the telegraph boy disappear. As she tore it open I locked my eyes shut. When I opened them she was reading the telegram and laughing. She walked to the bar and handed the wire to the sallow-faced bartender, the one we had driven home the night before. He read it without expression. Then he handed it to the other bartender. He, too, was unimpressed. I felt a deep gratitude for them. When Camilla read it again, I was grateful for that, too, but when she took it to a table where a group of men sat

71

drinking my mouth opened slowly and I was sick. The laughter of the men floated across the street. I shuddered and walked away quickly.

At Sixth I turned the corner and walked down to Main. I wandered through the crowds of seedy, hungry derelicts without destination. At Second I stopped before a Filipino taxi-dancehall. The literature on the walls spoke eloquently of forty beautiful girls and the dreamy music of Lonny Killula and his Melodic Hawaiians. I climbed one flight of echoing stairs to a booth and bought a ticket. Inside were the forty women, lined against the opposite wall, sleek in tight evening dresses, most of them blondes. Nobody was dancing, not a soul. On the platform the five-piece orchestra banged out a tune with fury. A few customers like myself stood behind a short wicker fence, opposite the girls. They beckoned to us. I surveyed the group, found a blonde whose gown I liked, and bought a few dance tickets. Then I waved at the blonde. She fell into my arms like an old lover and we beat the oak for two dances.

She talked soothingly and called me honey, but I thought only of that girl two streets away, of myself lying with her in the sand and making a fool of myself. It was useless. I gave the cloying blonde my handful of tickets and walked out of the hall and into the streets again. I could feel myself waiting, and when I kept looking at street clocks I knew what was wrong with myself. I was waiting for eleven o'clock, when the Columbia closed.

I was there at a quarter to eleven. I was there in the parking lot, walking toward her car. I sat on the burst upholstery and waited. Off in one corner of the parking lot was a shed where the attendant kept his accounts. Over the shed was a neon clock in red. I kept my eye on the clock, watched the minute hand rush toward eleven. Then I was afraid to see her again and as I squirmed and writhed in the seat my hand touched something soft. It was a cap of hers, a tam-o-shanter, it was black with a tiny fluffy knob on the crown. I felt it with my fingers and smelled it with my nose. Its powder was like herself. It was what I wanted. I stuffed it into my pocket and walked out of the parking lot. Then I climbed the stairs of Angel's Flight to my hotel. When I got to my room I took it out and threw it on the bed. I undressed, turned out the light, and held her hat in my arms.

Another day, poetry! Write her a poem, spill your heart to her in sweet cadences; but I didn't know how to write poetry. It was love and dove with me, bad rhymes, blundering sentiment. Oh Christ in Heaven, I'm no writer: I can't even put down a little quatrain, I'm no good in this world. I stood at the window and waved my hands at the sky; no good at all, just a cheap fake; neither writer nor lover; neither fish nor fowl.

Then what was the matter?

I had breakfast and went to a little Catholic Church at the edge of Bunker Hill. The rectory was in back of the frame church. I rang the bell and a woman in a nurse's apron answered. Her hands were covered with flour and dough.

"I want to see the pastor," I said.

The woman had a square jaw and a hostile pair of sharp grey eyes. "Father Abbot is busy," she said. "What do you want?"

"I have to see him," I said.

"I tell you he's busy."

The priest came to the door. He was stocky, powerful, smoking a cigar, a man in his fifties. "What is it?" he asked.

I told him I wanted to see him alone. I had some trouble on my mind. The woman sniffed contemptuously and disappeared through a hall. The priest opened the door and led me to his study. It was a small room crammed with books and magazines. My eyes bulged. There in one corner was a huge stack of Hackmuth's magazine. I walked to it at once and pulled out the issue containing *The Little Dog Laughed*. The priest had seated himself. "This is a great magazine," I said. "The greatest of them all."

The priest crossed his legs, shifted his cigar.

"It's rotten," he said. "Rotten to the core."

"I disagree," I said. "I happen to be one of its leading contributors."

"You?" the priest asked. "And what did you contribute?"

I spread *The Little Dog Laughed* before him on the desk. He glanced at it, pushed it aside. "I read that story," he said. "It's a piece of hogwash. And your reference to the Blessed Sacrament was a vile and contemptible lie. You ought to be ashamed of yourself."

Leaning back in his chair, he made it very plain that he didn't like me, his angry eyes centered on my forehead, his cigar rolling from one side of his mouth to the other.

"Now," he said. "What is it you wish to see me about?"

I didn't sit down. He made it very clear in his own way that I wasn't to use any of the furniture in the room. "It's about a girl," I said.

"What have you done to her?" he said.

"Nothing," I said. But I could speak no more. He had plucked out my heart. Hogwash! All those nuances, that superb dialogue, that brilliant lyricism—and he had called it hogwash. Better to close my ears and go away to some far off place where no words were spoken. Hogwash!

"I changed my mind," I said. "I don't want to talk about it now."

He stood up and walked toward the door.

"Very well," he said. "Good day."

I walked out, the hot sun blinding me. The finest short story in American Literature, and this person, this priest, had called it hogwash. Maybe that business about the Blessed Sacrament *wasn't* exactly true; maybe it didn't really happen. But my God, what psychological values! What prose! What sheer beauty!

As soon as I got to my room I sat down before my typewriter and planned my revenge. An article, a scathing attack upon the stupidity of the Church. I pecked out the title: *The Catholic Church Is Doomed.* I hammered it out furiously, one page after another, until there were six. Then I paused to read it. The stuff was awful, ludicrous. I tore it up and threw myself on the bed. I still hadn't written a poem to Camilla. As I lay there, inspiration came. I wrote it out from memory:

I have forgot much, Camilla! gone with the wind,
Flung roses, roses riotously with the throng,

74

Dancing, to put thy pale, lost lilies out of mind;
But I was desolate and sick with an old passion,
Yes, all the time, because the dance was long;
I have been faithful to thee, Camilla, in my fashion.
                                        Arturo Bandini.

I sent it by telegraph, proud of it, watched the telegraph clerk read it, beautiful poem, my poem to Camilla, a bit of immortality from Arturo to Camilla, and I paid the telegraph man and walked down to my place in the dark doorway, and there I waited. The same boy floated by on his bicycle. I watched him deliver it, watched Camilla read it in the middle of the floor, watched her shrug and rip it to pieces, saw the pieces floating to the sawdust on the floor. I shook my head and walked away. Even the poetry of Ernest Dowson had no effect upon her, not even Dowson.

Ah well, the hell with you Camilla. I can forget you. I have money. These streets are full of things you cannot give me. So down to Main Street and to Fifth Street, to the long dark bars, to the King Edward Cellar, and there a girl with yellow hair and sickness in her smile. Her name was Jean, she was thin and tubercular, but she was hard too, so anxious to get my money, her languid mouth for my lips, her long fingers at my trousers, her sickly lovely eyes watching every dollar bill.

"So your name is Jean," I said. "Well, well, well, a pretty name." We'll dance, Jean. We'll swing around, and you don't know it, you beauty in a blue gown, but you're dancing with a freak, an outcast from the world of man, neither fish, fowl, nor good red herring. And we drank and we danced and we drank again. Good fellow Bandini, so Jean called the boss. "This is Mr. Bandini. This is Mr. Schwartz." Very good, shake hands. "Nice place you got, Schwartz, nice girls."

One drink, two drinks, three drinks. What's that you're drinking Jean? I tasted it, that brownish stuff, looked like whiskey, must have been whiskey, such a face she made, her sweet face so contorted. But it wasn't whiskey, it was tea, plain tea, forty cents a slug. Jean, a little liar, trying to fool a great author. Don't fool me,

Jean. Not Bandini, lover of man and beast alike. So take this, five dollars, put it away, don't drink Jean, just sit here, only sit and let my eyes search your face because your hair is blonde and not dark, you are not like her, you are sick and you are from down there in Texas and you have a crippled mother to support, and you don't make very much money, only twenty cents a drink, you've only made ten dollars from Arturo Bandini tonight, you poor little girl, poor little starving girl with the sweet eyes of a baby and the soul of a thief. Go to your sailor boys, honey. They don't have the ten dollars but they've got what I haven't got, me, Bandini, neither fish, fowl nor good red herring, goodnight Jean, goodnight.

And here was another place and another girl. Oh, how lonely she was, from away back in Minnesota. A good family too. Sure, honey. Tell my tired ears about your good family. They owned a lot of property, and then the depression came. Well, how sad, how tragic. And now you work down here in a Fifth Street dive, and your name is Evelyn, poor Evelyn, and the folks are out here too, and you have the cutest sister, not like the tramps you meet down here, a swell girl, and you ask me if I want to meet your sister. Why not? She got her sister. Innocent little Evelyn went across the room and dragged poor little sister Vivian away from those lousy sailors and brought her to our table. Hello Vivian, this is Arturo. Hello Arturo, this is Vivian. But what happened to your mouth, Vivian, who dug it out with a knife? And what happened to your bloodshot eyes, and your sweet breath smelling like a sewer, poor kids, all the way from glorious Minnesota. Oh no, they're not Swedish, where did I get that idea? Their last name was Mortensen, but it wasn't Swedish, why their family had been Americans for generations. To be sure. Just a couple of home girls.

Do you know something?—Evelyn talking—Poor little Vivian had worked down here for almost six months and not once had any of these bastards ever ordered her a bottle of champagne, and I there, Bandini, I looked like such a swell guy, and wasn't Vivian cute, and wasn't it a shame, she so innocent, and would I buy her a bottle of champagne? Dear little Vivian, all the way from the clean fields of Minnesota, and not a Swede either, and almost a virgin too, just a few men short of being a virgin. Who could resist this tribute? So bring on the champagne, cheap champagne, just a pint size, we can all drink it, only eight dollars a bottle, and gee wasn't wine cheap out here? Why back in Duluth the champagne was twelve bucks a bottle.

Ah, Evelyn and Vivian, I love you both, I love you for your sad lives, the empty misery of your coming home at dawn. You too are alone, but you are not like Arturo Bandini, who is neither fish, fowl nor good red herring. So have your champagne, because I love you both, and you, too Vivian, even if your mouth looks like it had been dug out with raw fingernails and your old child's eyes swim in blood written like mad sonnets.

Chapter Eleven

But this was expensive. Take it easy, Arturo; have you forgotten those oranges? I counted what was left. It was twenty dollars and some cents. I was scared. I racked my brains over figures, added everything I had spent. Twenty dollars left—impossible! I had been robbed, I had misplaced the money, there was a mistake somewhere. I looked all over the room, burrowed into pockets and drawers, but that was all, and I was scared and worried and determined to go to work, write another one quick, something written so fast it had to be good. I sat before my typewriter and the great awful void descended, and I beat my head with my fists, put a pillow under my aching buttocks and made little noises of agony. It was useless. I had to see her, and I didn't care how I did it.

I waited for her in the parking lot. At eleven she came around the corner, and Sammy the bartender was with her. They both saw me from the distance and she lowered her voice, and when she got to the car Sammy said, "Hi there," but she said, "What do you want?"

"I want to see you," I said.

"I can't see you tonight," she said.

"Make it later on tonight."

"I can't. I'm busy."

"You're not that busy. You can see me."

She opened the car door for me to get out, but I did not move, and she said, "Please get out."

"Nothing doing," I said.

Sammy smiled. Her face flared.

"Get out, goddamnit!"

"I'm staying," I said.

"Come on, Camilla," Sammy said.

She tried to pull me out of the car, seized my sweater and jerked and tugged. "Why do you act like this?" she said. "Why can't you see I don't want to have anything to do with you?"

"I'm staying," I said.

"You fool!" she said.

Sammy had walked toward the street. She caught up with him and they walked away, and I was there alone, horrified, and smiling weakly at what I had done. As soon as they were out of sight I got out and walked up the stairs of the Flight and down to my room. I couldn't understand why I had done that. I sat on the bed and tried to push the episode out of my mind.

Then I heard a knock on my door. I didn't get a chance to say come in, because the door opened then and I turned around and there was a woman standing in the doorway, looking at me with a peculiar smile. She was not a large woman and she was not beautiful, but she seemed attractive and mature, and she had nervous black eyes. They were brilliant, the sort of eyes a woman gets from too much bourbon, very bright and glassy and extremely insolent. She stood in the door without moving or speaking. She was dressed intelligently: black coat with a furpiece, black shoes, black skirt, a white blouse and a small purse.

"Hello," I said.

"What are you doing?" she said.

"Just sitting here."

I was scared. The sight and nearness of that woman rather paralyzed me; maybe it was the shock of seeing her so suddenly, maybe it was my own misery at that moment, but the nearness of her and that crazy, glassy glitter of her eyes made me want to jump up and beat her, and I had to steady myself. The feeling lasted for only a moment, and then it was gone. She started across the room with those dark eyes insolently watching me, and I turned my face toward the window, not worried by her insolence but about that feeling which had gone through me like a bullet. Now there was the scent of perfume in the room, the perfume that floats after women in luxurious hotel lobbies, and the whole thing made me nervous and uncertain.

When she got close to me I didn't get up but sat still, took a long breath, and finally looked at her again. Her nose was pudgy at the end but it was not ugly and she had rather heavy lips without rouge, so that they were pinkish; but what got me were her eyes: their brilliance, their animalism and their recklessness.

She walked over to my desk and pulled a page out of the typewriter. I didn't know what was happening. I still said nothing, but I could smell liquor on her breath, and then the very peculiar but distinctive odor of decay, sweetish and cloying, the odor of oldness, the odor of this woman in the process of growing old.

She merely glanced at the script; it annoyed her and she flipped it over her shoulder and it zigzagged to the floor.

"It's no good," she said. "You can't write. You can't write at all."

"Thanks very much," I said.

I started to ask her what she wanted, but she did not seem the kind who accepts questions. I jumped off the bed and offered her the only chair in the room. She didn't want it. She looked at the chair and then at me, thoughtfully, smiling her disinterestedness in merely sitting down. Then she went around the room reading some stuff I had pasted on the walls. They were some excerpts I had typed from Mencken and from Emerson and Whitman. She sneered at them all. Poof, poof, poof! Making gestures with her fingers, curling her lips. She sat on the bed, pulled off her coat jacket to the elbows, and put her hands on her hips and looked at me with insufferable contempt.

Slowly and dramatically she began to recite:

> What should I be but a prophet and a liar,
> Whose mother was a leprechuan, whose father was a
>   friar?
> Teethed on a crucifix and cradled under water,
> What should I be but the fiend's god-daughter?

It was Millay, I recognized it at once, and she went on and on; she knew more Millay than Millay herself, and when she finally finished she lifted her face and looked at me and said, "That's *liter-*

ature! You don't know anything about literature. You're a fool!" I had fallen into the spirit of the lines and when she broke off so suddenly to denounce me I was at sea again.

I tried to answer but she interrupted and went off in a Barrymore manner, speaking deeply and tragically; murmuring of the pity of it all, the stupidity of it all, the absurdity of a hopelessly bad writer like myself buried in a cheap hotel in Los Angeles, California, of all places, writing banal things the world would never read and never get a chance to forget.

She lay back, laced her fingers under her head, and spoke dreamily to the ceiling: "You will love me tonight, you fool of a writer; yes, tonight you will love me."

I said, "Say, what *is* this, anyway?"

She smiled.

"Does it matter? You are nobody, and I might have been somebody, and the road to each of us is love."

The scent of her was pretty strong now, impregnating the whole room so that the room seemed to be hers and not mine, and I was a stranger in it, and I thought we had better go outside so she could get some of the night air. I asked her if she would like to walk around the block.

She sat up quickly. "Look! I have money, money! We will go somewhere and drink!"

"Sure thing!" I said. "A good idea."

I pulled on my sweater. When I turned around she was standing beside me, and she put the tips of her fingers on my mouth. That mysterious saccharine odor was so strong on her fingers that I walked toward the door and held it open and waited for her to pass through.

We walked upstairs and through the lobby. When we reached the front desk I was glad the landlady was gone to bed; there was no reason for it, but I didn't want Mrs. Hargraves to see me with this woman. I told her to tiptoe across the lobby, and she did it; she enjoyed it terribly, like an adventure in little things; it thrilled her and she tightened her fingers around my arm.

It was foggy on Bunker Hill, but not downtown. The streets

81

were deserted, and the sound of her heels on the sidewalk echoed among the old buildings. She tugged my arm and I bent down to hear what she wanted to whisper.

"You're going to be so marvelous!" she said. "So wonderful!"

I said, "Let's forget it now. Let's just walk."

She wanted a drink. She insisted upon it. She opened her purse and waved a ten dollar bill. "Look. Money! I have lots of money!"

We walked down to Solomon's Bar on the corner, where I played the pin games. Nobody was there but Solomon, who stood with his chin in his hands, worried about business. We walked to a booth facing the front window, and I waited for her to sit down, but she insisted I get in first. Solomon walked over for our order.

"Whiskey!" she said. "Lots of whiskey."

Solomon frowned.

"A short beer for me," I said.

Solomon was watching her sternly, searchingly, his bald spot crinkling from a frown. I could sense the consanguinity, and I knew then that she was Jewish too. Solomon went back for the drinks and she sat there with her eyes blazing, her hands folded on the table, her fingers twining and untwining. I sat trying to think of some way of dodging her.

"A drink'll fix you up fine," I said.

Before I knew it she was at my throat, but not roughly, her long fingernails and short fingers against my flesh as she talked about my mouth, my wonderful mouth; oh god, what a mouth I had.

"Kiss me!" she said.

"Sure," I said. "Let's have a drink first."

She clenched her teeth.

"Then you too know about me!" she said. "You're like the rest of them. You know about my wounds, and that's why you won't kiss me. Because I disgust you!"

I thought, she *is* crazy; I've got to get out of here. She kissed me, her mouth tasting of liverwurst on rye. She sat back, breathing with relief. I took out my handkerchief and wiped the sweat from my forehead. Solomon returned with the drinks. I reached for some money, but she paid quickly. Solomon went back for the change, but I called him back and handed him a bill. She fussed and protested, pounding her heels and fists. Solomon lifted his hands in a gesture of hopelessness and took her money. The moment his back was turned I said, "Lady, this is your party. I've got to go." She pulled me down and her arms went around me and we fought until I thought it was absurd. I sat back and tried to think of another escape.

Solomon brought back the change. I took a nickel from it and told her I'd like to play the pin game. Without a word she let me pass and I got up and walked over to the machine. She watched me like a prize dog, and Solomon watched her like a criminal. Then I won on the machine, and I called Solomon to come over and check the score.

I whispered, "Who is that woman, Solomon?"

He didn't know. She had been there earlier in the evening, drinking a great deal. I told him I wanted to go out the back way. "It's the door on the right," he said.

She finished her whiskey and hammered the table with the empty glass. I walked over, took a sip of beer, and told her to excuse me a minute. I jerked my thumb toward the men's room. She patted my arm. Solomon was watching me as I took the door opposite the men's room. It led to the storeroom, and the door to the alley was a few feet beyond. As soon as the fog smothered my face I felt better. I wanted to be as far away as possible. I wasn't hungry but I walked a mile to a hotdog stand on Eighth Street and had a cup of coffee to kill time. I knew she would go back to my room after she missed me. Something told me she was insane, it could have been that she had too much liquor, but it didn't matter, I didn't want to see her again.

I got back to my room at two in the morning. Her personality and that mysterious smell of old age still possessed it, and it was not my room at all. For the first time its wonderful solitude was spoiled. Every secret of that room seemed laid open. I threw open the two windows and watched the fog float through in sad tumbling lumps. When it got too cold I closed the windows and, though the room was wet from the fog and my papers and books were filmed with dampness, the perfume was still there unmistakably. I had Camilla's tam-o-shanter under my pillow. It too seemed drenched with the odor, and when I pressed it to my mouth it was like my mouth in that woman's black hair. I sat in front of the typewriter, idly tapping the keys.

As soon as I got started I heard steps in the hall and I knew she was coming back. I turned off the lights quickly and sat in the darkness, but I was too late, for she must have seen the light under the door. She knocked and I did not answer. She knocked again, but I sat still and puffed on a cigaret. Then she began to beat the door with her fists and she called out that she would start kicking it, and that she would kick it all night long, unless I opened it. Then she started kicking it, and it made a terrible noise through that rickety hotel, and I rushed over and opened the door.

"Darling!" she said, and she held out her arms.

"My God," I said. "Don't you think this has gone far enough? Can't you see I'm fed up?"

"Why did you leave me?" she asked. "Why did you do that?"

"I had another engagement."

"Darling," she said. "Why do you lie to me like that?"

"Oh nuts."

She walked across the room and pulled the page from my typewriter again. It was full of all manner of nonsense, a few odd phrases, my name written many times, bits of poetry. But this time her face broke into a smile.

"How wonderful!" she said. "You're a genius! My darling is so talented."

"I'm awfully busy," I said. "Will you please get out?"

It was as though she hadn't heard me. She sat on the bed, unbuttoned her jacket, and dangled her feet. "I love you," she said. "You're my darling, and you're going to love me."

I said, "Some other time. Not tonight. I'm tired."

That saccharine odor came through.

"I'm not kidding," I said. "I think you'd better go. I don't want to throw you out."

"I'm so lonely," she said.

She meant that. Something was wrong with her, twisted, gushing from her with those words, and I felt ashamed for being so harsh.

"Alright," I said. "We'll just sit here and talk for a while."

I pulled up the chair and straddled it, with my chin on the back, looking at her as she snuggled on the bed. She wasn't as drunk as I thought. Something was wrong with her and it was not alcohol and I wanted to find out what it was.

Her talk was madness. She told me her name, and it was Vera. She was a housekeeper for a rich Jewish family in Long Beach. But she was tired of being a housekeeper. She had come from Pennsylvania, fled across the country because her husband had been unfaithful to her. That day she had come down to Los Angeles from Long Beach. She had seen me in the restaurant on the corner of Olive Street and Second. She had followed me back to the hotel because my eyes "had pierced her soul." But I couldn't remember seeing her there. I was sure I had never seen her before. Having found out where I lived, she had gone to Solomon's and got drunk. All day she had been drinking, but it was only that she might become reckless and go to my room.

"I know how I revolt you," she said. "And that you know about my wounds and the horror my clothes conceal. But you must try to forget my ugly body, because I'm really good at heart, I'm so good, and I deserve more than your disgust."

I was speechless.

"Forgive my body!" she said. She put her arms out to me, the tears flowing down her cheeks. "Think of my soul!" she said. "My soul is so beautiful, it can bring you so much! It is not ugly like my flesh!"

She was crying hysterically, lying on her face, her hands groping through her dark hair, and I was helpless, I didn't know what she was talking about; ah, dear lady, don't cry like that, you mustn't cry like that, and I took her hot hand and tried to tell her she was talking in circles; it was all so silly, her talk, it was self-persecution, it was a lot of silly things, and I talked like that, gesturing with my hands, pleading with my voice.

"Because you're such a fine woman, and your body is so beautiful, and all this talk is an obsession, a childish phobia, a hangover from the mumps. So you mustn't worry and you mustn't cry, because you'll get over it. I know you will."

But I was clumsy, and making her suffer even more, because she was down in an inferno of her own creation, so far away from me that the sound of my voice made the hiatus seem worse. Then I tried to talk to her of other things, and I tried to make her laugh at my obsessions. Look lady, Arturo Bandini, he's got a few himself ! And from under the pillow I drew out Camilla's tam-o-shanter with the little tassle on it.

"Look lady! I've got them too. Do you know what I do, lady? I take this little black cap to bed with me, and I hold it close to me, and I say: 'Oh I love you, I love you, beautiful princess!'" And then I told her some more; oh, I was no angel; my soul had a few twists and bends all its own; so don't you feel so lonely, lady; because you've got lots of company; you've got Arturo Bandini, and he's got lots to tell you. And listen to this: Do you know what I did one night? Arturo, confessing it all: do you know the terrible thing I did? One night a woman too beautiful for this world came along on wings of perfume, and I could not bear it, and who she was I never knew, a woman in a red fox and a pert little hat, and Bandini trailing after her because she was better than dreams, watching her enter Bernstein's Fish Grotto, watching her in a trance through a window swimming with frogs and trout, watching her as she ate alone; and when she was through, do you know what I did, lady? So don't you cry, because you haven't heard anything yet, because I'm awful, lady, and my heart is full of black ink; me, Arturo Bandini, I walked right into Bernstein's Fish Grotto and I sat upon the very chair that she sat upon, and I shuddered with joy, and I fingered the napkin she had used, and there was a cigaret butt with a stain of lipstick upon it, and do you know what I did, lady? You with your funny little troubles, I ate the cigaret butt, chewed it up, tobacco and paper and all, swallowed it, and I thought it tasted fine, because she was so beautiful, and there was a spoon beside the plate, and I put it in my pocket, and every once in a while I'd take the spoon out of my pocket and taste it, because she was so beautiful. Love on a budget, a heroine free and for nothing, all for the black heart of Arturo Bandini, to be remembered through a window swimming with trout and frog legs. Don't you cry, lady; save your tears for Arturo Bandini, because he has his troubles, and they are great troubles, and I haven't even begun to talk, but I could say something to you about a night on the beach with a brown princess, and her flesh without meaning, her kisses like dead flowers, odorless in the garden of my passion.

But she was not listening, and she staggered off the bed, and she fell on her knees before me and begged me to tell her she was not disgusting.

"Tell me!" she sobbed. "Tell me I am beautiful like other women."

"Of course you are! You're really very beautiful!"

I tried to lift her, but she clung to me frantically, and I couldn't do anything but try to soothe her, but I was so clumsy, so inadequate, and she was so far down in the depths beyond me, but I kept trying.

Then she started again about her wounds, those ghastly wounds, they had wrecked her life, they had destroyed love before it came, driven a husband from her and into another woman's arms, and all of this was fantastic to me and incomprehensible because she was really handsome in her own way, she was not crippled and she was not disfigured, and there were plenty of men who would give her love.

She staggered to her feet and her hair had fallen to her face, the strands of hair pasted against her tear-soaked cheeks; her eyes were blotchy and she looked like a maniac, sodden with bitterness.

"I'll show you!" she screamed. "You'll see for yourself, you liar! liar!"

With both hands she jerked loose her dark skirt and it fell into a nest at her ankles. She stepped out of it and she was really beautiful in a white slip and I said it. I said, "But you're lovely! I told you you were lovely!"

She kept sobbing as she worked at the clasps of her blouse, and I told her it wasn't necessary to take off any more; she had convinced me beyond a doubt and there was no need for hurting herself further.

"No," she said. "You're going to see for yourself."

She couldn't release the clasps at the back of the blouse, and she backed toward me and told me to unclasp them. I waved my hand. "For God's sake, forget about it," I said. "You've convinced me. You don't have to do a strip act." She sobbed desperately and seized the thin blouse with her two hands and ripped it from her with one jerk.

When she began to lift her slip I turned my back and walked to the window, because I knew then she was going to show me something unpleasant, and she began to laugh at me and shriek at me and point her tongue at my worried face. "Ya, ya! See! You know already! You know all about them!"

I had to go through with it, and I turned around and she was nude except for hose and shoes, and then I saw the wounds. It was at the loins; it was a birthmark or something, a burn, a seared place, a pitiful, dry, vacant place where flesh was gone, where the thighs suddenly became small and shriveled and the flesh seemed dead. I closed my jaws and then I said, "What—that? Is that all, just that? It's nothing, a mere trifle." But I was losing the words, I had to say them quickly or they would never form. "It's ridiculous," I said. "I hardly noticed it. You're lovely; you're wonderful!"

She studied herself curiously, not believing me, and then she looked at me again, but I kept my eyes on her face, felt the floating nausea of my stomach, breathed the sweetish thickish odor of her presence, and I said again that she was beautiful, and the world slipped out like a whimper, so beautiful she was, a small girl, a virgin child, so beautiful and rare to behold, and without a word, and blushing, she picked up her slip and drew it over her head, a crooning and mysterious satisfaction in her throat.

She was so shy all at once, so delighted, and I laughed to find the words coming easier now, and I told her again and again of her loveliness, of how silly she had been. But say it fast, Arturo, say it quickly, because something was coming up in me, and I had to get out, so I told her I had to go down the hall a minute and for her to dress while I was gone. She covered herself and her eyes were swimming in joy as she watched me leave. I went down to the end of the hall to the landing of the fire-escape, and there I let go, crying and unable to stop because God was such a dirty crook, such a contemptible skunk, that's what he was for doing that thing to that woman. Come down out of the skies, you God, come on down and I'll hammer your face all over the city of Los Angeles, you miserable unpardonable prankster. If it wasn't for you, this woman would not be so maimed, and neither would the world, and if it wasn't for you I could have had Camilla Lopez down at the beach, but no! You have to play your tricks: see what you have done to this woman, and to the love of Arturo Bandini for Camilla Lopez. And then my tragedy seemed greater than the woman's, and I forgot her.

When I got back she was dressed and combing her hair in front of the little mirror. The torn blouse was stuffed inside her coat pocket. She seemed so exhausted and yet so serenely happy, and I told her I would walk downtown with her to the Electric Depot, where she would catch a train for Long Beach. She told me no, I wouldn't have to do that. She wrote out her address on a piece of paper.

"Some day you'll come to Long Beach," she said. "I will wait a long time, but you'll come."

At the door we said goodbye. She held out her hand, it was so warm and alive. "Goodbye," she said. "Take care of yourself."

"Goodbye, Vera."

There was no solitude after she left, there was no escape from that strange scent. I lay down and even Camilla who was a pillow with a tam-o-shanter for a head seemed so far away and I could not bring her back. Slowly I felt myself filling with desire and sadness; you could have had her, you fool, you could have done what you pleased, just like Camilla, and you didn't do anything. All through the night she mangled my sleep. I would wake up to breathe the sweet heaviness she had left behind, and touch the furniture she had touched, and think of the poetry she had recited. When I fell asleep I had no recollection of it, for when I awoke it was ten in the morning and I was still tired, sniffing the air and thinking restlessly of what had happened. I could have said so much to her, and she would have been so kind. I could have said, look Vera, such and such is the situation, and such and such happened, and if you could do such and such, perhaps it would not happen again, because such and such a person thinks such and such about me, and it's got to stop; I shall die trying, but it's got to stop.

So I sit around all day thinking about it; and I think about a few other Italians, Casanova and Cellini, and then I think about Arturo Bandini, and I have to punch myself in the head. I begin to wonder about Long Beach, and I say to myself that perhaps I should at least visit the place, and maybe Vera, to have a talk with her concerning a great problem. I think of that cadaverous place, the wound on her body, and try to find words for it, to fit it across the page of a manuscript. Then I say to myself that Vera, for all her flaws, might perform a miracle, and after the miracle is performed a new Arturo Bandini will face the world and Camilla Lopez, a Bandini with dynamite in his body and volcanic fire in his eyes, who goes to this Camilla Lopez and says: see here, young woman, I have been very patient with you, but now I have had enough of your impudence, and you will kindly oblige me by removing your clothes. These vagaries please me as I lie there and watch them unfold across the ceiling.

One afternoon I tell Mrs. Hargraves that I shall be gone for a day or so, Long Beach, some business, and I start out. I have Vera's address in my pocket, and I say to myself, Bandini, prepare yourself for the great adventure; let the conquering spirit possess you. On the corner I meet Hellfrick, whose mouth is watering for more meat. I give him some money and he dashes into a butcher shop. Then I go down to the Electric Station and catch a Red Car for Long Beach.

Chapter Twelve

The name on the mailbox was Vera Rivken, and that was her full name. It was down on the Long Beach Pike, across the street from the Ferris Wheel and the Roller Coaster. Downstairs a poolhall, upstairs a few single apartments. No mistaking that flight of stairs; it possessed her odor. The banister was warped and bent, and the grey wallpaint was swollen, with puffed places that cracked open when I pushed them with my thumb.

When I knocked, she opened the door.

"So soon?" she said.

Take her in your arms, Bandini. Don't grimace at her kiss, break away gently, with a smile, say something. "You look wonderful," I said. No chance to speak, she was over me again, clinging like a wet vine, her tongue like a frightened snake's head, searching my mouth. Oh great Italian Lover Bandini, reciprocate! Oh Jewish girl, if you would be so kind, if you would approach these matters more slowly! So I was free again, wandering to the window, saying something about the sea and the view beyond. "Nice view," I said. But she was taking off my coat, leading me to a chair in the corner, taking off my shoes. "Be comfortable," she said. Then she was gone, and I sat with my teeth gritted, looking at a room like ten million California rooms, a bit of wood here and a bit of rag there, the furniture, with cobwebs in the ceiling and dust in the corners, her room, and everybody's room, Los Angeles, Long Beach, San Diego, a few boards of plaster and stucco to keep the sun out.

She was in a little white hole called the kitchen, scattering pans and rattling glasses, and I sat and wondered why she could be one thing when I was alone in my room and something else the moment I was with her. I looked for incense, that saccharine smell, it had to come from somewhere, but there was no incense burner in the room, nothing in the room but dirty blue overstuffed furniture, a table with a few books scattered over it, and a mirror over the paneling of a Murphy bed. Then she came out of the kitchen with a glass of milk in her hand. "Here," she offered. "A cool drink."

But it wasn't cool at all, it was almost hot, and there was a yellowish scum on the top, and sipping it I tasted her lips and the strong food she ate, a taste of rye bread and Camembert cheese. "It's good," I said, "delicious."

She was sitting at my feet, her hands on my knees, staring at me with the eyes of hunger, tremendous eyes so large I might have lost myself in them. She was dressed as I saw her the first time, the same clothes, and the place was so desolate I knew she had no others, but I had come before she had had a chance to powder or rouge and now I saw the sculpture of age under her eyes and through her cheeks. I wondered that I had missed these things that night, and then I remembered that I had not missed them at all, I had seen them even through rouge and powder, but in the two days of reverie and dream about her they had concealed themselves, and now I was here, and I knew I should not have come.

We talked, she and I. She asked about my work and it was a pretense, she was not interested in my work. And when I answered it was a pretense. I was not interested in my work either. There was only one thing that interested us, and she knew it, for I had made it plain by my coming.

But where were all the words, and where were all the little lusts I had brought with me? And where were those reveries, and where was my desire, and what had happened to my courage, and why did I sit and laugh so loudly at things not amusing? So come, Bandini—find your heart's desire, take your passion the way it says in the books. Two people in a room; one of them a woman; the other, Arturo Bandini, who is neither fish, fowl, nor good red herring.

Another long silence, the woman's head on my lap, my fingers playing in the dark nest, sorting out strands of grey hair. Awake, Arturo! Camilla Lopez should see you now, she with the big black eyes, your true love, your Mayan princess. Oh Jesus, Arturo, you're marvelous! Maybe you did write *The Little Dog Laughed*, but you'll never write Casanova's Memoirs. What are you doing, sitting here? Dreaming of some great masterpiece? Oh you fool, Bandini!

She looked up at me, saw me there with eyes closed, and she didn't know my thoughts. But maybe she did. Maybe that was why she said, "You're tired. You must take a nap." Maybe that was why she pulled down the Murphy bed and insisted that I lie upon it, she beside me, her head in my arms. Maybe, studying my face, that was why she asked, "You love somebody else?"

I said, "Yes. I'm in love with a girl in Los Angeles."

She touched my face.

"I know," she said. "I understand."

"No you don't."

Then I wanted to tell her why I had come, it was right there at the tip of my tongue, springing to be told, but I knew I would never speak of that now. She lay beside me and we watched the emptiness of the ceiling, and I played with the idea of telling her. I said, "There's something I want to tell you. Maybe you can help me out." But I got no farther than that. No, I could not say it to her; but I lay there hoping she would somehow find out for herself, and when she kept asking me what it was that bothered me I knew she was handling it wrong, and I shook my head and made impatient faces. "Don't talk about it," I said. "It's something I can't tell you."

"Tell me about her," she said.

I couldn't do that, be with one woman and speak of the wonders of another. Maybe that was why she asked, "Is she beautiful?" I answered that she was. Maybe that was why she asked, "Does she love you?" I said she didn't love me. Then my heart pounded in my throat, because she was coming nearer and nearer to what I wanted her to ask, and I waited while she stroked my forehead.

"And why doesn't she love you?"

There it was. I could have answered and it would have been in the clear, but I said, "She just doesn't love me, that's all."

"Is it because she loves somebody else?"

"I don't know. Maybe."

Maybe this and maybe that, questions, questions, wise, wounded woman, groping in the dark, searching for the passion of Arturo Bandini, a game of hot and cold, with Bandini eager to give it away. "What is her name?"

"Camilla," I said.

She sat up, touched my mouth.

"I'm so lonely," she said. "Pretend that I am she."

"Yes," I said. "That's it. That's your name. It's Camilla."

I opened my arms and she sank against my chest.

"My name is Camilla," she said.

"You're beautiful," I said. "You're a Mayan princess."

"I am Princess Camilla."

"All of this land and this sea belongs to you. All of California. There is no California, no Los Angeles, no dusty streets, no cheap hotels, no stinking newspapers, no broken, uprooted people from the East, no fancy boulevards. This is your beautiful land with the desert and the mountains and the sea. You're a princess, and you reign over it all."

"I am Princess Camilla," she sobbed. "There are no Americans, and no California. Only deserts and mountains and the sea, and I reign over it all."

"Then I come."

"Then you come."

"I'm myself. I'm Arturo Bandini. I'm the greatest writer the world ever had."

"Ah yes," she choked. "Of course! Arturo Bandini, the genius of the earth." She buried her face in my shoulder and her warm tears fell on my throat. I held her closer. "Kiss me, Arturo."

But I didn't kiss her. I wasn't through. It had to be my way or nothing. "I'm a conqueror," I said. "I'm like Cortez, only I'm an Italian."

I felt it now. It was real and satisfying, and joy broke through me, the blue sky through the window was a ceiling, and the whole living world was a small thing in the palm of my hand. I shivered with delight.

"Camilla, I love you so much!"

There were no scars, and no desiccated place. She was Camilla, complete and lovely. She belonged to me, and so did the world. And I was glad for her tears, they thrilled me and lifted me, and I possessed her. Then I slept, serenely weary, remembering vaguely through the mist of drowsiness that she was sobbing, but I didn't care. She wasn't Camilla anymore. She was Vera Rivken, and I was in her apartment and I would get up and leave just as soon as I had some sleep.

She was gone when I woke up. The room was eloquent with her departure. A window open, curtains blowing gently. A closet door ajar, a coat-hanger on the knob. The half-empty glass of milk where I had left it on the arm of the chair. Little things accusing Arturo Bandini, but my eyes felt cool after sleep and I was anxious to go and never come back. Down in the street there was music from a merry-go-round. I stood at the window. Below two women passed, and I looked down upon their heads.

Before leaving I stood at the door and took one last look around the room. Mark it well, for this was the place. Here too history was made. I laughed. Arturo Bandini, suave fellow, sophisticated; you should hear him on the subject of women. But the room seemed so poor, pleading for warmth and joy. Vera Rivken's room. She had been nice to Arturo Bandini, and she was poor. I took the small roll from my pocket, peeled off two one dollar bills, and laid them on the table. Then I walked down the stairs, my lungs full of air, elated, my muscles so much stronger than ever before.

But there was a tinge of darkness in the back of my mind. I walked down the street, past the Ferris Wheel and canvassed concessions, and it seemed to come stronger; some disturbance of peace, something vague and nameless seeping into my mind. At a hamburger stand I stopped and ordered coffee. It crept upon me—the restlessness, the loneliness. What was the matter? I felt my pulse. It was good. I blew on the coffee and drank it: good coffee. I searched, felt the fingers of my mind reaching out but not quite touching whatever it was back there that bothered me. Then it came to me like crashing and thunder, like death and destruction. I got up from the counter and walked away in fear, walking fast down the boardwalk, passing people who seemed strange and ghostly: the world seemed a myth, a transparent plane, and all things upon it were here for only a little while; all of us, Bandini, and Hackmuth and Camilla and Vera, all of us were here for a little while, and then we were somewhere else; we were not alive at all; we approached living, but we never achieved it. We are going to die. Everybody was going to die. Even you, Arturo, even you must die.

I knew what it was that swept over me. It was a great white cross pointing into my brain and telling me I was a stupid man, because I was going to die, and there was nothing I could do about it. *Mea culpa, mea culpa, mea maxima culpa.* A mortal sin, Arturo. Thou shalt not commit adultery. There it was, persistent to the end, assuring me that there was no escape from what I had done. I was a Catholic. This was a mortal sin against Vera Rivken.

At the end of the row of concessions the sand beach began. Beyond were dunes. I waded through the sand to a place where the dunes hid the boardwalk. This needed thinking out. I didn't kneel; I sat down and watched the breakers eating the shore. This is bad, Arturo. You have read Nietzsche, you have read Voltaire, you should know better. But reasoning wouldn't help. I could reason myself out of it, but that was not my blood. It was my blood that kept me alive, it was my blood pouring through me, telling me it was wrong. I sat there and gave myself over to my blood, let it carry me swimming back to the deep sea of my beginnings. Vera Rivken, Arturo Bandini. It was not meant that way: it was never meant that way. I was wrong. I had committed a mortal sin. I could figure it mathematically, philosophically, psychologically: I could prove it a dozen ways, but I was wrong, for there was no denying the warm even rhythm of my guilt.

Sick in my soul I tried to face the ordeal of seeking forgiveness. From whom? What God, what Christ? They were myths I once believed, and now they were beliefs I felt were myths. This is the sea, and this is Arturo, and the sea is real, and Arturo believes it real. Then I turn from the sea, and everywhere I look there is land;

I walk on and on, and still the land goes stretching away to the horizons. A year, five years, ten years, and I have not seen the sea. I say unto myself, but what has happened to the sea? And I answer, the sea is back there, back in the reservoir of memory. The sea is a myth. There never was a sea. But there *was* a sea! I tell you I was born on the seashore! I bathed in the waters of the sea! It gave me food and it gave me peace, and its fascinating distances fed my dreams! No, Arturo, there never was a sea. You dream and you wish, but you go on through the wasteland. You will never see the sea again. It was a myth you once believed. But, I have to smile, for the salt of the sea is in my blood, and there may be ten thousand roads over the land, but they shall never confuse me, for my heart's blood will ever return to its beautiful source.

Then what shall I do? Shall I lift my mouth to the sky, stumbling and burbling with a tongue that is afraid? Shall I open my chest and beat it like a loud drum, seeking the attention of my Christ? Or is it not better and more reasonable that I cover myself and go on? There will be confusions, and there will be hunger; there will be loneliness with only my tears like wet consoling little birds, tumbling to sweeten my dry lips. But there shall be consolation, and there shall be beauty like the love of some dead girl. There shall be some laughter, a restrained laughter, and quiet waiting in the night, a soft fear of the night like the lavish, taunting kiss of death. Then it will be night, and the sweet oils from the shores of my sea, poured upon my senses by the captains I deserted in the dreamy impetuousness of my youth. But I shall be forgiven for that, and for other things, for Vera Rivken, and for the ceaseless flapping of the wings of Voltaire, for pausing to listen and watch that fascinating bird, for all things there shall be forgiveness when I return to my homeland by the sea.

I got up and plodded through the deep sand toward the boardwalk. It was the full ripeness of evening, with the sun a defiant red ball as it sank beyond the sea. There was something breathless about the sky, a strange tension. Far to the south sea gulls in a black mass roved the coast. I stopped to pour sand from my shoes, balanced on one leg as I leaned against a stone bench.

Suddenly I felt a rumble, then a roar.

The stone bench fell away from me and thumped into the sand. I looked at the row of concessions: they were shaking and cracking. I looked beyond to the Long Beach skyline; the tall buildings were swaying. Under me the sand gave way; I staggered, found safer footing. It happened again.

It was an earthquake.

Now there were screams. Then dust. Then crumbling and roaring. I turned round and round in a circle. I had done this. I had done this. I stood with my mouth open, paralyzed, looking about me. I ran a few steps toward the sea. Then I ran back.

You did it, Arturo. This is the wrath of God. You did it.

The rumbling continued. Like a carpet over oil, the sea and land heaved. Dust rose. Somewhere I heard a booming of debris. I heard screams, and then a siren. People running out of doors. Great clouds of dust.

You did it, Arturo. Up in that room on that bed you did it.

Now the lamp posts were falling. Buildings cracked like crushed crackers. Screams, men shouting, women screaming. Hundreds of people rushing from buildings, hurrying out of danger. A woman lying on the sidewalk, beating it. A little boy crying. Glass splintering and shattering. Fire bells. Sirens. Horns. Madness.

Now the big shake was over. Now there were tremors. Deep in the earth the rumbling continued. Chimneys toppled, bricks fell and a grey dust settled over all. Still the temblors. Men and women running toward an empty lot away from buildings.

I hurried to the lot. An old woman wept among the white faces. Two men carrying a body. An old dog crawling on his belly, dragging his hind legs. Several bodies in the corner of the lot, beside a shed, blood-soaked sheets covering them. An ambulance. Two high school girls, arms locked, laughing. I looked down the street. The building fronts were down. Beds hung from walls. Bathrooms were exposed. The street was piled with three feet of debris. Men were shouting orders. Each temblor brought more tumbling debris. They stepped aside, waited, then plunged in again.

I had to go. I walked to the shed, the earth quivering under me. I opened the shed door, felt like fainting. Inside were bodies in a row, sheets over them, blood oozing through. Blood and death. I walked off and sat down. Still the temblors, one after another.

Where was Vera Rivken? I got up and walked to the street. It had been roped off. Marines with bayonets patroled the roped area. Far down the street I saw the building where Vera lived. Hanging from the wall, like a man crucified, was the bed. The floor was gone and only one wall stood erect. I walked back to the lot. Somebody had built a bonfire in the middle of the lot. Faces reddened in the blaze. I studied them, found nobody I knew. I didn't find Vera Rivken. A group of old men were talking. The tall one with the beard said it was the end of the world; he had predicted it a week before. A woman with dirt smeared over her hair broke into the group. "Charlie's dead," she said. Then she wailed. "Poor Charlie's dead. We shouldn't have to come! I told him we shouldn't a come!" An old man seized her by the shoulders, swung her around. "What the hell you sayin'?" he said. She fainted in his arms.

I went off and sat on the curbing. Repent, repent before it's too late. I said a prayer but it was dust in my mouth. No prayers. But there would be some changes made in my life. There would be decency and gentleness from now on. This was the turning point. This was for me, a warning to Arturo Bandini.

Around the bonfire the people were singing hymns. They were in a circle, a huge woman leading them. Lift up thine eyes to Jesus, for Jesus is coming soon. Everybody was singing. A kid with a monogram on his sweater handed me a hymn book. I walked over. The woman in the circle swung her arms with wild fervor, and the song tumbled with the smoke toward the sky. The temblors kept coming. I turned away. Jesus, these Protestants! In my church we didn't sing cheap hymns. With us it was Handel and Palestrina.

It was dark now. A few stars appeared. The temblors were ceaseless, coming every few seconds. A wind rose from the sea and it grew cold. People huddled in groups. From everywhere sirens sounded. Above, airplanes droned, and detachments of sailors and marines poured through the streets. Stretcher-bearers dashed into ruined buildings. Two ambulances backed toward the shed. I got up and walked away. The Red Cross had moved in. There was an emergency headquarters at one corner of the lot. They were handing out big tins of coffee. I stood in line. The man ahead of me was talking.

"It's worse in Los Angeles," he said. "Thousands dead."

Thousands. That meant Camilla. The Columbia Buffet would be the first to tumble. It was so old, the brick walls so cracked and feeble. Sure, she was dead. She worked from four until eleven. She had been caught in the midst of it. She was dead and I was alive. Good. I pictured her dead: she would lie still in this manner; her eyes closed like this, her hands clasped like that. She was dead and I was alive. We didn't understand one another, but she had been good to me, in her fashion. I would remember her a long time. I was probably the only man on earth who would remember her. I could think of so many charming things about her; her huaraches, her shame for her people, her absurd little Ford.

All sorts of rumors circulated through the lot. A tidal wave was coming. A tidal wave wasn't coming. All of California had been struck. Only Long Beach had been struck. Los Angeles was a mass of ruins. They hadn't felt it in Los Angeles. Some said the dead numbered fifty thousand. This was the worst quake since San Francisco. This was much worse than the San Francisco quake. But in spite of it all, everybody was orderly. Everybody was frightened, but it was not a panic. Here and there people smiled: they were brave people. They were a long way from home, but they brought their bravery with them. They were tough people. They weren't afraid of anything.

The marines set up a radio in the middle of the lot, with big loudspeakers yawning into the crowd. The reports came through constantly, outlining the catastrophe. The deep voice bellowed instructions. It was the law and everybody accepted it gladly. Nobody was to enter or leave Long Beach until further notice. The city was under martial law. There wasn't going to be a tidal wave. The danger was definitely over. The people were not to be alarmed by the temblors, which were to be expected, now that the earth was settling once more.

The Red Cross passed out blankets, food, and lots of coffee. All night we sat around the loudspeaker, listening to developments. Then the report came that the damage in Los Angeles was negligible. A long list of the dead was broadcast. But there was no Camilla Lopez on the list. All night I swallowed coffee and smoked cigarets, listening to the names of the dead. There was no Camilla; not even a Lopez.

Chapter Thirteen

I got back to Los Angeles the next day. The city was the same, but I was afraid. The streets lurked with danger. The tall buildings forming black canyons were traps to kill you when the earth shook. The pavement might open. The street cars might topple. Something had happened to Arturo Bandini. He walked the streets of one-story buildings. He clung to the curbstone, away from the overhanging neon signs. It was inside me, deeply. I could not shake it. I saw men walking through deep, dark alleys. I marveled at their madness. I crossed Hill Street and breathed easier when I entered Pershing Square. No tall buildings in the Square. The earth could shake, but no debris could crush you.

I sat in the Square, smoked cigarets and felt sweat oozing from my palms. The Columbia Buffet was five blocks away. I knew I would not go down there. Somewhere within me was a change. I was a coward. I said it aloud to myself: you are a coward. I didn't care. It was better to be a live coward than a dead madman. These people walking in and out of huge concrete buildings—someone should warn them. It would come again; it had to come again, another earthquake to level the city and destroy it forever. It would happen any minute. It would kill a lot of people, but not me. Because I was going to keep out of these streets, and away from falling debris.

I walked up Bunker Hill to my hotel. I considered every building. The frame buildings could stand a quake. They merely shook and writhed, but they did not come down. But look out for the brick places. Here and there were evidences of the quake; a tumbled brick wall, a fallen chimney. Los Angeles was doomed. It was a city with a curse upon it. This particular earthquake had not destroyed it, but any day now another would raze it to the ground.

They wouldn't get me, they'd never catch me inside a brick building. I was a coward, but that was my business. Sure I'm a coward, talking to myself, sure I'm a coward, but you be brave, you lunatic, go ahead and be brave and walk around under those big buildings. They'll kill you. Today, tomorrow, next week, next year, but they'll kill you and they won't kill me.

And now listen to the man who was in the earthquake. I sat on the porch of the Alta Loma Hotel and told them about it. I saw it happen. I saw the dead carried out. I saw the blood and the wounded. I was in a six-story building, fast asleep when it happened. I ran down the corridor to the elevator. It was jammed. A woman rushed out of one of the offices and was struck on the head by a steel girder. I fought my way back through the ruins and got to her. I slung her over my shoulders, it was six floors to the ground, but I made it. All night I was with the rescuers, knee deep in blood and misery. I pulled an old woman out whose hand stuck through the debris like a piece of statue. I flung myself through a smoking doorway to rescue a girl unconscious in her bathtub. I dressed the wounded, led battalions of rescuers into the ruins, hacked and fought my way to the dead and dying. Sure I was scared, but it had to be done. It was a crisis, calling for action and not words. I saw the earth open like a huge mouth, then close again over the paved street. An old man was trapped by the foot. I ran to him, told him to be brave while I hacked the pavement with a fireman's axe. But I was too late. The vise tightened, bit his leg off at the knee. I carried him away. His knee is still there, a bloody souvenir sticking out of the earth. I saw it happen, and it was awful. Maybe they believed me, maybe they didn't. It was all the same to me.

I went down to my room and looked for cracks in the wall. I inspected Hellfrick's room. He was stooped over his stove, frying a pan of hamburger. I saw it happen, Hellfrick. I was atop the highest point of the Roller Coaster when the quake hit. The Coaster jammed in its tracks. We had to climb down. A girl and myself. A hundred and fifty feet to the ground, with a girl on my back and the structure shaking like St. Vitus Dance. I made it though. I saw a little girl buried feet first in debris. I saw an old woman pinned under her car, dead and crushed, but holding her hand out to signal for a right hand turn. I saw three men dead at a poker table. Hellfrick whistled: is that so? Is that so? Too bad, too bad. And would I lend him fifty cents? I gave it to him and inspected his walls for cracks. I went down the halls, into the garage and laundry room. There were evidences of the shock, not serious, but indicative of the calamity that would inevitably destroy Los Angeles. I didn't sleep in my room that night. Not with the earth still trembling. Not me, Hellfrick. And Hellfrick looked out the window to where I lay on the hillside, wrapped in blankets. I was crazy, Hellfrick said. But Hellfrick remembered that I had been lending him money, so maybe I wasn't crazy. Maybe you're right, Hellfrick said. He turned out his light and I heard his thin body settle upon the bed.

The world was dust, and dust it would become. I began going to Mass in the mornings. I went to Confession. I received Holy Communion. I picked out a little frame church, squat and solid, down near the Mexican quarter. Here I prayed. The new Bandini. Ah life! Thou sweet bitter tragedy, thou dazzling whore that leadeth me to destruction! I gave up cigarets for a few days. I bought a new rosary. I poured nickels and dimes into the Poor Box. I pitied the world.

Dear Mother back home in Colorado. Ah, beloved character, so like the Virgin Mary. I only had ten dollars left, but I sent her five of it, the first money I ever sent home. Pray for me, Mother dear. The vigil of your rosaries is all that keeps my blood astir. These are dark days, Mother. The world is so full of ugliness. But I have changed, and life has begun anew. Long hours I spend glorying thee before God. Ah mother, be with me in these miseries! But I must hasten to close this epistle, Oh, beloved Mother Darling, for I am making a *novena* these days, and each afternoon at five I am to be found prostrate before the figure of Our Blessed Savior as I offer prayers for His sweet Mercy. Farewell, O Mother! Heed my plea for your aspirations. Remember me to Him that giveth all and shineth in the skies.

So off to mail the letter to my mother, to drop it in the box and walk down Olive Street, where there were no brick buildings, and then across an empty lot and down another street that was barren of buildings to a street where only a low fence marked the spot, and then a block to a section of town where high buildings rose to the sky; but there was no escaping that block, save to walk across the street from the high buildings, walk very fast, sometimes run. And at the end of the street was the little church, and here I prayed, making my *novena*.

An hour later I come out, refreshed, soothed, spirits high. I take the same route home, hurry past the high buildings, stroll along the fence, dawdle through the empty lot, taking note of God's handiwork in a line of palm trees near the alley. And so up to Olive Street, past the drab frame houses. What doth it profit a man if he gain the whole world and suffer the loss of his own soul? And then that little poem: Take all the pleasures of all the spheres, multiply them by endless years, one minute of heaven is worth them all. How true! How true! I thank thee, Oh heavenly light, for showing the way.

A knock on the window. Someone was knocking on the window of that house obscured by heavy vines. I turned and found the window, saw a head; the flash of teeth, the black hair, the leer, the gesturing long fingers. What was that thunder in my belly? And how shall I prevent that paralysis of thought, and that inundation of blood making my senses reel? But I want this! I shall die without it! So I'm coming you woman in the window; you fascinate me, you kill me dead with delight and shudder and joy, and here I come, up these rickety stairs.

So what's the use of repentence, and what do you care for goodness, and what if you *should* die in a quake, so who the hell cares? So I walked downtown, so these were the high buildings, so let the earthquake come, let it bury me and my sins, so who the hell cares? No good to God or man, die one way or another, a quake or a hanging, it didn't matter why or when or how.

And then, like a dream it came. Out of my desperation it came—an idea, my first sound idea, the first in my entire life, full-bodied and clean and strong, line after line, page after page. A story about Vera Rivken.

I tried it and it moved easily. But it was not thinking, not cogitation. It simply moved of its own accord, spurted out like blood. This was it. I had it at last. Here I go, leave me be, oh boy do I love it, Oh God do I love you, and you Camilla and you and you. Here I go and it feels so good, so sweet and warm and soft, delicious, delirious. Up the river and over the sea, this is you and this is me, big fat words, little fat words, big thin words, whee whee whee.

Breathless, frantic, endless thing, going to be something big, going on and on, I hammered away for hours, until gradually it came upon me in the flesh, stole over me, haunted my bones, dripped from me, weakened me, blinded me. Camilla! I had to have that Camilla! I got up and walked out of the hotel and down Bunker Hill to the Columbia Buffet.

"Back again?"
Like film over my eyes, like a spider web over me.
"Why not?"

Arturo Bandini, author of *The Little Dog Laughed* and a certain plagiarization from Ernest Dowson, and a certain telegram proposing marriage. Could that be laughter in her eyes? But forget it, and remember the dark flesh under her smock. I drank beer and watched her at work. I sneered when she laughed with those men near the piano. I cackled when one of them put his hand on her hip. This Mexican! Trash, I tell you! I signalled her. She came at her leisure, fifteen minutes later. Be nice to her, Arturo. Fake it.

"You want something else?"
"How are you, Camilla?"
"Alright, I guess."
"I'd like to see you after work."
"I have another engagement."
Gently: "Could you postpone it, Camilla? It's very important that I see you."

"I'm sorry."

"Please, Camilla. Just tonight. It's so important."

"I can't, Arturo. Really, I can't."

"You'll see me," I said.

She walked away. I pushed back my chair. I pointed my finger at her, yelled it out: "You'll see me! You little insolent beerhall twirp! You'll see me!"

You're goddamn right she'd see me. Because I was going to wait. Because I walked out to the parking lot and sat on the running board of her car and waited. Because she wasn't so good that she could excuse herself from a date with Arturo Bandini. Because, by God, I hated her guts.

Then she came into the lot, and Sammy the bartender was with her. She paused when she saw me get to my feet. She put her hand on Sammy's arm, restraining him. They whispered. Then it was going to be a fight. Fine. Come you, you stupid scarecrow of a bartender, just you make a pass at me and I'll break you in half. And I stood there with both fists hard and waiting. They approached. Sammy didn't speak. He walked around me and got into the car. I stood beside the driver's seat. Camilla looked straight ahead, opened the car door. I shook my head.

"You're going with me, Mexican."

I seized her wrist.

"Let go!" she said. "Get your filthy hands off!"

"You're going with me."

Sammy leaned over.

"Maybe she doesn't feel like it, kid."

I had her with my right hand. I raised my left fist and shoved it against Sammy's face. "Listen," I said. "I don't like you. So keep that lousy trap shut."

"Be sensible," he said. "What for you want to get all burned up about a dame?"

"She's going with me."

"I'm *not* going with you!"

She tried to pass. I grabbed her arms and flung her like a dancer. She went spinning across the lot, but she did not fall. She screamed, charged me. I caught her in my arms and pinned her elbows down. She kicked and tried to scratch my legs. Sammy watched with disgust. Sure I was disgusting, but that was my affair. She cried and fought, but she was helpless, her legs dangling, her arms held tight. Then she tired a little, and I released her. She straightened her dress, her teeth chattering her hatred.

"You're going with me," I said.

Sammy got out of the car.

"This is terrible," he said. He took Camilla's arm and led her toward the street. "Let's get out of here."

I watched them go. He was right. Bandini, the idiot, the dog, the skunk, the fool. But I couldn't help it. I looked at the car certificate and found her address. It was a place near 24th and Alameda. I couldn't help it. I walked to Hill Street and got aboard an Alameda trolley. This interested me. A new side to my character, the bestial, the darkness, the unplumbed depth of a new Bandini. But after a few blocks the mood evaporated. I got off the car near the freight yards. Bunker Hill was two miles away, but I walked back. When I got home I said I was through with Camilla Lopez forever. And you'll regret it, you little fool, because I'm going to be famous. I sat before my typewriter and worked most of the night.

I worked hard. It was supposed to be Autumn, but I couldn't tell the difference. We had sun every day, blue skies every night. Sometimes there was fog. I was eating fruit again. The Japanese gave me credit and I had the pick of their stalls. Bananas, oranges, pears, plums. Once in a while I ate celery. I had a full can of tobacco and a new pipe. There wasn't any coffee, but I didn't mind. Then my new story hit the magazine stands. *The Long Lost Hills!* It was not as exciting as *The Little Dog Laughed*. I scarcely looked at the free copy Hackmuth sent me. This pleased me nevertheless. Some day I would have so many stories written I wouldn't remember where they appeared. "Hi there, Bandini! Nice story you had in *The Atlantic Monthly* this month." Bandini puzzled. "Did I have one in the *Atlantic?* Well, well."

Hellfrick the meat-eater, the man who never paid his just debts. So much I had lent him during that lush period, but now that I was poor again he tried to barter with me. An old raincoat, a pair of slippers, a box of fancy soap—these he offered me for payment. I refused them. "My God, Hellfrick. I need money, not secondhand goods." His meat craze had got out of hand. All day I heard him frying cheap steaks, the odor creeping under my door. It gave me a mad desire for meat. I would go to Hellfrick. "Hellfrick," I would say. "How about sharing that steak with me?" The steak would be so large it filled the skillet. But Hellfrick would lie brazenly. "I haven't had a thing for two days." I would call him violent names; soon I lost all respect for him. He would shake his red, bloated face, big eyes staring pitifully. But he never offered me so much as the scraps from his plate. Day after day I worked, writhing from the tantalizing odor of fried pork chops, grilled steaks, fried steaks, breaded steaks, liver and onions, and all manner of meats.

One day his craze for meat was gone, and the craze for gin returned. He was steadily drunk for two nights. I could hear him stumbling about, kicking bottles and talking to himself. Then he went away. He was gone another night. When he returned, his pension check was spent, and he had somehow, somewhere, he did not remember it, bought a car. We went behind the hotel and looked at this car. It was a huge Packard, more than twenty years old. It stood there like a hearse, the tires worn, the cheap black paint bubbling in the hot sun. Somebody down on Main Street had sold it to him. Now he was broke, with a big Packard on his hands.

"You want to buy it?" he said.

"Hell, no."

He was dejected, his head bursting from a hangover.

That night he walked into my room. He sat on the bed, his long arms dangling to the floor. He was homesick for the middle-west. He talked of rabbit-hunting, of fishing, of the good old days when he was a kid. Then he began on the subject of meat. "How would you like a big thick steak?" he said, his lips loose. He opened two fingers. "Thick as that. Broiled. Lots of butter over it. Burned just enough to give it a tang. How would you like it?"

"I'd love it."

He got up.

"Then come on, and we'll get one."

"You got money?"

"We don't need any money. I'm hungry."

I grabbed my sweater and followed him down the hall to the alley. He got into his car. I hesitated. "Where you going, Hellfrick?"

"Come on," he said. "Leave it to me."

I got in beside him.

"No trouble," I said.

"Trouble!" he sneered. "I tell you I know where to get us a steak."

We drove in moonlight out Wilshire to Highland, then out Highland over Cahuenga Pass. On the other side lay the flat plain of the San Fernando Valley We found a lonely road off the pavement and followed it through tall eucalyptus trees to scattered farmhouses and pasture lands. After a mile the road ended. Barbed wire and fence posts appeared in the glare of headlights. Hellfrick laboriously turned the car around, faced it toward the pavement from which we had detoured. He got out of the front seat, opened the rear door, and fumbled with car tools under the rear cushion.

I leaned over and watched him.

"What's up, Hellfrick?"

He stood up, a jackhammer in his hand.

"You wait here."

He stopped under a loop in the barbed wire and crossed the pasture. A hundred yards away a barn loomed in the moonlight. Then I knew what he was after. I jumped out of the car and called to him. He shushed me angrily. I watched him tiptoe toward the barn door. I cursed him and waited tensely. In a little while I heard the mooing of a cow. It was a piteous cry. Then I heard a thud and a scuffle of hoofs. Out of the barn door came Hellfrick. Across his shoulder lay a dark mass, weighing him down. Behind him, mooing continually, a cow followed. Hellfrick tried to run, but the dark mass beat him down to a fast walk. Still the cow pursued, pushing her nose into his back. He turned around, kicked wildly. The cow stopped, looked toward the barn, and mooed again.

"You fool, Hellfrick. You goddamn fool!"

"Help me," he said.

I raised the loose barbed wire to a width that would permit him and his burden to pass under. It was a calf, blood spurting from a gash between the ears. The calf's eyes were wide open. I could see the moon reflected in them. It was coldblooded murder. I was sick and horrified. My stomach twisted when Hellfrick dumped the calf into the back seat. I heard the body thump, and then the head. I was sick, very sick. It was plain murder.

All the way home Hellfrick was exultant, but the steering wheel was sticky with blood, and once or twice I thought I heard the calf kicking in the back seat. I held my face in my hands and tried to forget the melancholy call of the calf's mother, the sweet face of the dead calf. Hellfrick drove very fast. On Beverly we shot by a black car moving slowly. It was a police cruiser. I gritted my teeth and waited for the worst. But the police did not follow us. I was too sick to be relieved. One thing was certain: Hellfrick was a murderer, he and I were through. On Bunker Hill we turned down our alley and pulled up at the parking space adjacent the hotel wall. Hellfrick got out.

"Now I'm going to give you a lesson in butchering."

"You are like hell," I said.

I acted as lookout for him as he wrapped the calf's head in newspapers, slung it over his shoulder, and hurried down the dim hallway to his room. I spread newspapers over his dirty floor, and he lowered the calf upon them. He grinned at his bloody trousers his bloody shirt, his bloody arms.

I looked down at the poor calf. Its hide was spotted black and white and it had the most delicate ankles. From the slightly open mouth there appeared a pink tongue. I closed my eyes and ran out Hellfrick's room and threw myself on the floor in my room. I lay there and shuddered, thinking of the old cow alone in the field in the moonlight, old cow mooing for her calf. Murder! Hellfrick and I were through. He didn't have to pay back the debt. It was blood money—not for me.

After that night I was very cold toward Hellfrick. I never visited his room again. A couple of times I recognized his knock, but I kept the door bolted so he couldn't barge in. Meeting in the hall, we merely grunted. He owed me almost three dollars, but I never did collect it.

Chapter Fourteen

Good news from Hackmuth. Another magazine wanted *The Long Lost Hills* in digest form. A hundred dollars. I was rich again. A time for amends, for righting the past. I sent my mother five dollars. I cried when she sent me a letter of thanks. The tears rolled down my eyes as I quickly replied. And I sent five more. I was pleased with myself. I had a few good qualities. I could see them, my biographers, talking to my mother, a very old lady in a wheel chair: he was a good son, my Arturo, a good provider.

Arturo Bandini, the novelist. Income of his own, made it writing short stories. Writing a book now. Tremendous book. Advance notices terrific. Remarkable prose. Nothing like it since Joyce. Standing before Hackmuth's picture, I read the work of each day. I spent whole hours writing a dedication: To J. C. Hackmuth, for discovering me. To J. C. Hackmuth, in admiration. To Hackmuth, a man of genius. I could see them, those New York critics, crowding Hackmuth at his club. You certainly found a winner in that Bandini kid on the coast. A smile from Hackmuth, his eyes twinkling.

Six weeks, a few sweet hours every day, three and four and sometimes five delicious hours, with the pages piling up and all other desires asleep. I felt like a ghost walking the earth, a lover of man and beast alike, and wonderful waves of tenderness flooded me when I talked to people and mingled with them in the streets. God Almighty, dear God, good to me, gave me a sweet tongue, and these sad and lonely folk will hear me and they shall be happy. Thus the days passed. Dreamy, luminous days, and sometimes such great quiet joy came to me that I would turn out my lights and cry, and a strange desire to die would come to me.

Thus Bandini, writing a novel.

One night I answered a knock on my door, and there she stood.

"Camilla!"

She came in and sat down on the bed, something under her arm, a bundle of papers. She looked at my room: so this was where I lived. She had wondered about the place I lived. She got up and walked around, peering out the window, walking around the room, beautiful girl, tall Camilla, warm dark hair, and I stood and watched her. But why had she come? She felt my question, and she sat on the bed and smiled at me.

"Arturo," she said. "Why do we fight all the time?"

I didn't know. I said something about temperaments, but she shook her head and crossed her knees, and a sense of her fine thighs being lifted lay heavily in my mind, thick suffocating sensation, warm lush desire to take them in my hands. Every move she made, the soft turn of her neck, the large breasts swelling under the smock, her fine hands upon the bed, the fingers spread out, these things disturbed me, a sweet painful heaviness dragging me into stupor. Then the sound of her voice, restrained, hinting of mockery, a voice that talked to my blood and bones. I remembered the peace of those past weeks, it seemed so unreal, it had been a hypnotism of my own creation, because this was being alive, this looking into the black eyes of Camilla, matching her scorn with hope and a brazen gloating.

She had come for something else beside a mere visit. Then I found out what it was.

"You remember Sammy?"

Of course.

"You didn't like him."

"He was alright."

"He's good, Arturo. You'd like him if you knew him better."

"I suppose."

"He liked you."

I doubted that, after the scuffle in the parking lot. I remembered certain things about her relationship with Sammy, her smiles for him during work, her concern the night we took him home. "You love that guy, don't you?"

"Not exactly."

She took her eyes off my face and let them travel around the room.

"Yes you do."

All at once I loathed her, because she had hurt me. This girl! She had torn up my sonnet by Dowson, she had shown my telegram to everybody in the Columbia Buffet. She had made a fool of me at the beach. She suspected my virility, and her suspicion was the same as the scorn in her eyes. I watched her face and lips and thought how it would be a pleasure to strike her, send my fist with all force against her nose and lips.

She spoke of Sammy again. Sammy had had all the rotten breaks in life. He might have been somebody, except that his health had always been poor.

"What's the matter with him?"

"T. B." she said.

"Tough."

"He won't live long."

I didn't give a damn.

"We all have to die someday."

I thought of throwing her out, saying to her: if you've come here to talk about that guy, you can get the hell out because I'm not interested. I thought that would be delightful: order her out, she so wonderfully beautiful in her own way, and forced to leave because I ordered her out.

"Sammy's not here any more. He's gone."

If she thought I was curious about his whereabouts, she was badly mistaken. I put my feet on the desk and lit a cigaret.

"How are all your other boy friends?" I said. It had bolted out of me. I was sorry at once. I softened it with a smile. The corners of her lips responded, but with an effort.

"I haven't any boy friends," she said.

"Sure," I said, touching it slightly with sarcasm. "Sure, I understand. Forgive an incautious remark."

She was silent for a while. I made a pretense at whistling. Then she spoke: "Why are you so mean?" she said.

"Mean?" I said. "My dear girl, I am equally fond of man and beast alike. There is not the slightest drop of enmity in my system. After all, you can't be mean and still be a great writer."

Her eyes mocked me. "Are you a great writer?"

"That's something you'll never know."

She bit her lower lip, pinched it between two white sharp teeth, looking toward the window and the door like a trapped animal, then smiled again. "That's why I came to see you."

She fumbled with the big envelopes on her lap, and it excited me, her own fingers touching her lap, lying there and moving against her own flesh. There were two envelopes. She opened one of them. It was a manuscript of some sort. I took it from her hands. It was a short story by Samuel Wiggins, General Delivery, San Juan, California. It was called 'Coldwater Gatling,' and it began like this: "Coldwater Gatling wasn't looking for trouble but you never can tell about those Arizona rustlers. Pack your cannon high on the hip and lay low when you seen one of them babies. The trouble with trouble was that trouble was looking for Coldwater Gatling. They don't like Texas Rangers down in Arizona, consequently Coldwater Gatling figured shoot first and find out who you killed afterwards. That's how they did it in the Lone Star State where men were men and the women didn't mind cooking for hard-riding straight-shooting people like Coldwater Gatling, the toughest man in leather they had down there."

That was the first paragraph.

"Hogwash," I said.

"Please help him."

He was going to die in a year, she said. He had left Los Angeles and gone to the edge of the Santa Ana desert. There he lived in a shack, writing feverishly. All his life he had wanted to write. Now, with such little time remaining, his chance had come.

"What's in it for me?" I said.

"But he's dying."

"Who isn't?"

I opened the second manuscript. It was the same sort of stuff. I shook my head. "It stinks."

116

"I know," she said. "But couldn't you do something to it? He'll give you half the money."

"I don't need money. I have an income of my own."

She rose and stood before me, her hands on my shoulders. She lowered her face, her warm breath sweet in my nostrils, her eyes so large they reflected my head in them and I felt delirious and sick with desire. "Would you do it for me?"

"For you?" I said. "Well, for you—yes."

She kissed me. Bandini, the stooge. Thick, warm kiss, for services about to be rendered. I pushed her away carefully. "You don't have to kiss me. I'll do what I can." But I had an idea or two of my own on the subject, and while she stood at the mirror and rouged her lips I looked at the address on the manuscripts. San Juan, California. "I'll write him a letter about this stuff," I said. She watched me through the mirror, paused with the lipstick in her hand. Her smile was mocking me. "You don't have to do that," she said. "I could come back and pick them up and mail them myself."

That was what she said, but you can't fool me, Camilla, because I can see your memories of that night at the beach written upon your scornful face, and do I hate you, oh God how I loathe you!

"Okay," I said. "I guess that would be best. You come back tomorrow night."

She was sneering at me. Not her face, her lips, but from within her. "What time shall I come?"

"What time are you through work?"

She turned around, snapped her purse shut, and looked at me. "You know what time I'm through work," she said.

I'll get you, Camilla. I'll get you yet.

"Come then," I said.

She walked to the door, put her hand on the knob.

"Goodnight, Arturo."

"I'll walk up to the lobby with you."

"Don't be silly," she said.

The door closed. I stood in the middle of the room and listened to her footsteps on the stairs. I could feel the whiteness of my face,

117

the awful humiliation, and I got mad and I reached my hair with my fingers and howled out of my throat as I pulled at my hair, loathing her, beating my fists together, lurching around the room with arms clasped against myself, struggling with the hideous memory of her, choking her out of my consciousness, gasping with hatred.

But there were ways and means, and that sick man out in the desert was going to get his too. I'll get you, Sammy. I'll cut you to pieces, I'll make you wish you were dead and buried a long time ago. The pen is mightier than the sword, Sammy boy, but the pen of Arturo Bandini is mightier still. Because my time has come, Sir. And now you get yours.

I sat down and read his stories. I made notes on every line and sentence and paragraph of it. The writing was pretty terrible, a first effort, clumsy stuff, vague, jerky, absurd. Hour after hour I sat there consuming cigarets and laughing wildly at Sammy's efforts, gloating over them, rubbing my hands together gleefully. Oh boy, would I lay him low! I jumped up and strutted around the room, shadow-boxing: take that, Sammy boy, and that, and how do you like this left hook, and how do you like this right cross, zingo, bingo, bang, biff, blooey!

I turned around and saw the crease on the bed where Camilla had been seated, the sensuous contour where her thighs and hips had sunk beneath the softness of the blue chenille bedspread. Then I forgot Sammy, and wild with longing I threw myself upon my knees before the spot and kissed it reverently.

"Camilla, I love you!"

And when I had worn the sensation to vaporous nothingness, I got up, disgusted with myself, black awful Arturo Bandini, black vile dog.

I sat down and grimly went to work on my letter of criticism to Sammy.

Dear Sammy:
That little whore was here tonight; you know, Sammy, the little Greaser dame with a wonderful figure and a mind for a moron. She presented me with certain alleged

118

writings purportedly written by yourself. Furthermore she stated the man with the scythe is about to mow you under. Under ordinary circumstances I would call this a tragic situation. But having read the bile your manuscripts contain, let me speak for the world at large and say at once that your departure is everybody's good fortune. You can't write, Sammy. I suggest you concentrate on the business of putting your idiotic soul in order these last days before you leave a world that sighs with relief at your departure. I wish I could honestly say that I hate to see you go. I wish too that, like myself, you could endow posterity with something like a monument to your days upon this earth. But since this is so obviously impossible, let me urge you to be without bitterness in your final days. Destiny has indeed been unkind to you. Like the rest of the world, I suppose you too are glad that in a short time all will be finished, and the ink spot you have splattered will never be examined from a larger view. I speak for all sensible, civilized men when I urge you to burn this mass of literary manure and thereafter stay away from pen and ink. If you have a typewriter, the same holds true; because even the typing in this manuscript is a disgrace. If, however, you persist in your pitiful desire to write, by all means send me the pap you compose. I found at least you are amusing. Not deliberately, of course.

There it was, finished, devastating. I folded the manuscripts, placed the note with them inside a big envelope, sealed it, addressed it to Samuel Wiggins, General Delivery, San Juan, California, stamped it, and shoved it into my back pocket. Then I went upstairs and out of the lobby to the mailbox on the corner. It was a little after three o'clock of an incomparable morning. The blue and white of stars and sky were like desert colors, a gentleness so stirring I had to pause and wonder that it could be so lovely. Not a blade of the dirty palms stirred. Not a sound was to be heard.

All that was good in me thrilled in my heart at that moment, all that I hoped for in the profound, obscure meaning of my existence. Here was the endlessly mute placidity of nature, indifferent to the great city; here was the desert beneath these streets, around these streets, waiting for the city to die, to cover it with timeless sand once more. There came over me a terrifying sense of understanding about the meaning and the pathetic destiny of men. The desert was always there, a patient white animal, waiting for men to die, for civilizations to flicker and pass into the darkness. Then men seemed brave to me, and I was proud to be numbered among them. All the evil of the world seemed not evil at all, but inevitable and good and part of that endless struggle to keep the desert down.

I looked southward in the direction of the big stars, and I knew that in that direction lay the Santa Ana desert, that under the big stars in a shack lay a man like myself, who would probably be swallowed by the desert sooner than I, and in my hand I held an effort of his, an expression of his struggle against the implacable silence toward which he was being hurled. Murderer or bartender or writer, it didn't matter: his fate was the common fate of all, his finish my finish; and here tonight in this city of darkened windows were other millions like him and like me: as indistinguishable as dying blades of grass. Living was hard enough. Dying was a supreme task. And Sammy was soon to die.

I stood at the mailbox, my head against it, and grieved for Sammy, and for myself, and for all the living and the dead. Forgive me, Sammy! Forgive a fool! I walked back to my room and spent three hours writing the best criticism of his work I could possibly write. I didn't say that this was wrong or that was wrong. I kept saying, in my opinion this would be better if, and so forth, and so forth. I got to sleep about six o'clock, but it was a grateful, happy sleep. How wonderful I really was! A great, soft-spoken, gentle man, a lover of all things, men and beast alike.

Chapter Fifteen

I didn't see her again for a week. In the meantime I got a letter from Sammy, thanking me for the corrections. Sammy, her true love. He also sent some advice: how was I getting along with the Little Spick? She wasn't a bad dame, not bad at all when the lights were out, but the trouble with you, Mr. Bandini, is that you don't know how to handle her. You're too nice to that girl. You don't understand Mexican women. They don't like to be treated like human beings. If you're nice to them, they walk all over you.

I worked on the book, pausing now and then to re-read his letter. I was reading it the night she came again. It was about midnight, and she walked in without knocking.

"Hello," she said.

I said, "Hello, Stupid."

"Working?" she said.

"What does it look like?" I said.

"Mad?" she said.

"No," I said. "Just disgusted."

"With me?"

"Naturally," I said. "Look at yourself."

Under her jacket was the white smock. It was spotted, stained. One of her stockings was loose, wrinkled at the ankles. Her face seemed tired, some of the lip rouge having vanished. The coat she wore was dotted with lint and dust. She was perched on cheap high heels.

"You try so hard to be an American," I said. "Why do you do that? Take a look at yourself."

She went to the mirror, studied herself gravely. "I'm tired," she said. "We were busy tonight."

"It's those shoes," I said. "You ought to wear what your feet were

121

meant to wear—huaraches. And all that paint on your face. You look awful—a cheap imitation of an American. You look frowsy. If I were a Mexican I'd knock your head off. You're a disgrace to your people."

"Who are you to talk like that?" she said. "I'm just as much an American as you are. Why, you're not an American at all. Look at your skin. You're dark like Eyetalians. And your eyes, they're black."

"Brown," I said.

"They're not either. They're black. Look at your hair. Black."

"Brown," I said.

She took off her coat, threw herself on the bed and stuck a cigaret in her mouth. She began to fumble and search for a match. There was a pack beside me on the desk. She waited for me to hand them to her.

"You're not crippled," I said. "Get them yourself."

She lit her cigaret and smoked in silence, her stare at the ceiling, smoke tumbling from her nostrils in quiet agitation. It was foggy outside. Far away came the sound of a police siren.

"Thinking of Sammy?" I said.

"Maybe."

"You don't have to think of him here. You can always leave, you know."

She snubbed out the cigaret, twisted and gutted it and her words had the same effect. "Jesus, you're nasty," she said. "You must be awfully unhappy."

"You're crazy."

She lay with her legs crossed. The tops of her rolled stockings and an inch or two of dark flesh showed where the white smock ended. Her hair spilled over the pillow like a bottle of overturned ink. She lay on her side, watching me out of the depth of the pillow. She smiled. She lifted her hand and wagged her finger at me.

"Come here, Arturo," she said. It was a warm voice.

I waved my hand.

"No thanks. I'm comfortable."

For five minutes she watched me stare through the window. I

might have touched her, held her in my arms; yes, Arturo, it was only a matter of getting out of the chair and stretching out beside her, but there was the night at the beach and the sonnet on the floor and the telegram of love and I remembered them like nightmares filling the room.

"Scared?" she said.

"Of you?" I laughed.

"You are," she said.

"No I'm not."

She opened her arms and all of her seemed to open to me, but it only closed me deeper into myself, carrying with me the image of her at that time, how lush and soft she was.

"Look," I said. "I'm busy. Look." I patted the pile of manuscript beside the typewriter.

"You're afraid, too."

"Of what?"

"Me."

"Pooh."

Silence.

"There's something wrong with you," she said.

"What?"

"You're queer."

I got up and stood over her.

"That's a lie," I said.

We lay there. She was forcing it with her scorn, the kiss she gave me, the hard curl of her lips, the mockery of her eyes, until I was like a man made of wood and there was no feeling within me except terror and a fear of her, a sense that her beauty was too much, that she was so much more beautiful than I, deeper rooted than I. She made me a stranger unto myself, she was all of those calm nights and tall eucalyptus trees, the desert stars, that land and sky, that fog outside, and I had come there with no purpose save to be a mere writer, to get money, to make a name for myself and all that piffle. She was so much finer than I, so much more honest, that I was sick of myself and I could not look at her warm eyes, I suppressed the shiver brought on by her brown arms around my neck and the long fingers in my hair. I did not kiss her. She kissed me, author of *The Little Dog Laughed.* Then she took my wrist with her two hands. She pressed her lips into the palm of my hand. She placed my hand upon her bosom between her breasts. She turned her lips toward my face and waited. And Arturo Bandini, the great author dipped deep into his colorful imagination, romantic Arturo Bandini, just chock-full of clever phrases, and he said, weakly, kittenishly, "Hello."

"Hello?" she answered, making a question of it. "Hello?" And she laughed. "Well, how are you?"

Oh that Arturo! That spinner of tales.

"Swell," he said.

And now what? Where was the desire and the passion? She would go away in a little while and then it would come. But my God, Arturo. You can't *do* that! Recall your marvelous predecessors! Measure to your standards. I felt her groping hands, and I groped to discourage them, to hold them in passionate fear. Once more she kissed me. She might have given her lips to a cold boiled ham. I was miserable.

She pushed me away.

"Get away," she said. "Let me go."

The disgust, the terror and humiliation burned in me, and I would not let go. I clung to her, forced the cold of my mouth against her warmth, and she fought with me to break away, and I lay there holding her, my face in her shoulder, ashamed to show it. Then I felt her scorn grow to hatred as she struggled, and it was then that I wanted her, held her and pleaded with her, and with each wrench of her black rage my desire mounted and I was happy, saying hooray for Arturo, joy and strength, strength through joy, the delicious sense of it, the rapturous self-satisfaction, the delight to know that I could possess her now if I wished. But I did not wish it, for I had had my love. Dazzled I had been by the power and joy of Arturo Bandini. I released her, took my hand from her mouth, and jumped off the bed.

She sat there, the white of saliva at the ends of her mouth, her teeth gritted, her hands pulling at her long hair, her face fighting off a scream, but it didn't matter; she could scream if she liked, for Arturo Bandini wasn't queer, there was nothing at all wrong with Arturo Bandini; why, he had a passion like six men, that boy, he had felt it coming to the surface: some guy, mighty writer, mighty lover; right with the world, right with his prose.

I watched her straighten her dress, watched her stand up, panting and frightened, and go to the mirror and look at herself, as though to make sure it was really herself.

"You're no good," she said.

I sat down and chewed on a fingernail.

"I thought you were something else," she said. "I hate rough stuff."

Rough stuff: pooh. What did it matter what she thought? The big thing was proved: I could have had her, and whatever she thought was not important. I was something else besides a great writer: I was no longer afraid of her: I could look into her face as a man should look into the face of a woman. She left without speaking again. I sat in a dream of delight, an orgy of comfortable confidence: the world was so big, so full of things I could master. Ah, Los Angeles! Dust and fog of your lonely streets, I am no longer lonely. Just you wait, all of you ghosts of this room, just you wait, because it will happen yet, and that Camilla, she can have her Sammy in the desert, with his cheap short stories and stinking prose, but wait until she has a taste of me, because it will happen, as sure as there's a God in heaven.

I don't remember. Maybe a week passed, maybe two weeks. I knew she would return. I did not wait. I lived my life. I wrote a few pages. I read a few books. I was serene: she would come back. It would be at night. I never thought of her as a thing to be considered by daylight. The many times I had seen her, none had been in the day. I expected her like I expected the moon.

She did come. This time I heard pebbles plinking off my windowpane. I opened the window wide, and there she stood on the hillside, a sweater over her white apron. Her mouth was open slightly as she gazed up at me.

"What you doing?" she said.

"Just sitting here."

"You mad at me?"

"No. You mad at me?"

She laughed. "A little."

"Why?"

"You're mean."

We went for a ride. She asked if I knew anything about guns. I didn't. We drove to a shooting gallery on Main Street. She was an expert shot. She knew the proprietor, a kid in a leather jacket. I couldn't hit anything, not even the big target in the middle. It was her money, and she was disgusted with me. She could hold a revolver under her armpit and hit the bull's eye of the big target. I took about fifty shots, and missed every time. Then she tried to show me how to hold the gun. I jerked it away from her, flung the barrel recklessly in all directions. The kid in the leather jacket ducked under the counter. "Be careful!" he yelled. "Look out!"

Her disgust became humiliation. She dug a fifty cent piece out of her pocketful of tips. "Try again," she said. "And this time, don't miss, or I won't pay for it." I didn't have any money with me. I put the gun down on the counter and refused to shoot again. "To hell with it," I said.

"He's a sissy, Tim," she said. "All he can do is write poetry."

Tim obviously liked only people who knew how to shoot a gun. He looked at me with distaste, saying nothing. I picked up a repeating Winchester rifle, took aim, and started pumping lead. The big target sixty feet away, three feet above the ground on a post, showed no sign of being hit. A bell was supposed to ring when the bull's eye was hit. Not a sound. I emptied the gun, sniffed the tart stench of powder, and made a face. Tim and Camilla laughed at the sissy. By now a crowd had gathered on the sidewalk. They all shared Camilla's disgust, for it was a contagious thing, and I felt it too. She turned, saw the crowd, and blushed. She was ashamed of me, annoyed and mortified. Out of the side of her mouth she whispered to me that we should leave. She broke through the crowd, walking fast, six feet ahead of me. I followed leisurely. Ho ho, and what did I care if I couldn't shoot a damned gun, and what did I care if those mugs had laughed, and that she had laughed, for which one of them, the boobish swine, the lousy grinning Main Street dopes, which one of them could compose a story like *The Long Lost Hills?* Not a one of them! And so to hell with their scorn.

The car was parked in front of a cafe. When I reached it she had already started the engine. I got in but she did not wait for me to get seated. Still sneering, she looked at me quickly, and let out the clutch. I was thrown against the seat, then against the windshield. We were jammed between two other cars. She banged into one, and then into the other, her way of letting me know what a fool I had been. When we finally broke from the curb and swung into the street, I sighed and sat back.

"Thank God for that," I said.

"You dry up!" she said.

"Look," I said. "If you have to feel this way, why don't you just let me out. I can walk."

She immediately put her foot on the throttle. We raced through the downtown streets. I sat hanging on and thought of jumping. Then we reached a section where the traffic was sparse. We were two miles from Bunker Hill, in the east part of town, in the section of factories and breweries. She slowed the car down and pulled up to the curb. We were along side of a low black fence. Beyond it were stacks of steel pipe.

"Why here?" I said.

"You wanted to walk," she said. "Get out and walk."

"I feel like riding again."

"Get out," she said. "I mean it, too. Anybody that can't shoot any better than that! Go on, get out!"

I reached for my cigarets, offered her one.

"Let's talk this over," I said.

She slapped the pack of cigarets out of my hand, knocked them to the floor, and glared at me defiantly. "I hate you," she said. "God, how I hate you!"

As I picked up the cigarets the night and the deserted factory district quivered with her loathing. I understood it. She did not hate Arturo Bandini, not really. She hated the fact that he did not meet her standard. She wanted to love him, but she couldn't. She wanted him like Sammy: quiet, taciturn, grim, a good shot with a rifle, a good bartender who accepted her as a waitress and nothing else. I got out of the car, grinning, because I knew that would hurt her.

"Good night," I said. "It's a fine night. I don't mind walking."

"I hope you never make it," she said. "I hope they find you dead in the gutter in the morning."

"I'll see what I can do," I said.

As she drove away a sob came from her throat, a cry of pain. One thing was certain: Arturo Bandini was not good for Camilla Lopez.

Chapter Sixteen

The good days, the fat days, page upon page of manuscript; prosperous days, something to say, the story of Vera Rivken, and the pages mounted and I was happy. Fabulous days, the rent paid, still fifty dollars in my wallet, nothing to do all day and night but write and think of writing: ah, such sweet days, to see it grow, to worry for it, myself, my book, my words, maybe important, maybe timeless, but mine nevertheless, the indomitable Arturo Bandini, already deep into his first novel.

So an evening comes, and what to do with it, my soul so cool from the bath of words, my feet so solid upon the earth, and what are the others doing, the rest of the people of the world? I will go sit and look at her, Camilla Lopez.

It was done. It was like old times, our eyes springing at one another. But she was changed, she was thinner, and her face was unhealthy, with two eruptions at each end of her mouth. Polite smiles. I tipped her and she thanked me. I fed the phonograph nickels, playing her favorite tunes. She wasn't dancing at her work, and she didn't look at me often the way she used to. Maybe it was Sammy: maybe she missed the guy.

I asked her, "How is he?"

A shrug: "Alright, I guess."

"Don't you see him?"

"Oh, sure."

"You don't look well."

"I feel alright."

I got up. "Well, I gotta go. Just dropped in to see how you were getting along."

"It was nice of you."

"Not at all. Why don't you come and see me?"

She smiled. "I might, some night."

Dear Camilla, you did come finally. You threw pebbles at the window, and I pulled you into the room, smelled the whiskey on your breath, and puzzled while you sat slightly drunk at my typewriter, giggling while you played with the keyboard. Then you turned to look at me, and I saw your face clearly under the light, the swollen lower lip, the purple and black smudge around your left eye.

"Who hit you?" I said. And you answered, "Automobile accident." And I said, "Was Sammy driving the other car?" And you wept, drunk and heartbroken. I could touch you then and not fuss with desire. I could lie beside you on the bed and hold you in my arms and hear you say that Sammy hated you, that you drove out to the desert after work, and that he slugged you twice for waking him up at three in the morning.

I said, "But why see him?"

"Because I'm in love with him."

You got a bottle from your purse and we drank it up; first your turn, then mine. When the bottle was empty I went down to the drugstore and bought another, a big bottle. All night we wept and we drank, and drunk I could say the things bubbling in my heart, all those swell words, all the clever similes, because you were crying for the other guy and you didn't hear a word I said, but I heard them myself, and Arturo Bandini was pretty good that night, because he was talking to his true love, and it wasn't you, and it wasn't Vera Rivken either, it was just his true love. But I said some swell things that night, Camilla. Kneeling beside you on the bed, I held your hand and I said, "Ah Camilla, you lost girl! Open your long fingers and give me back my tired soul! Kiss me with your mouth because I hunger for the bread of a Mexican hill. Breathe the fragrance of lost cities into fevered nostrils, and let me die here, my hand upon the soft contour of your throat, so like the whiteness of some half-forgotten southern shore. Take the longing in these restless eyes and feed it to lonely swallows cruising an Autumn cornfield, because I love you Camilla, and your name is

130

sacred like that of some brave princess who died with a smile for a love that was never returned."

I was drunk that night, Camilla, drunk on seventy-eight cent whiskey, and you were drunk on whiskey and grief. I remember that after turning off the lights, naked except for one shoe that baffled me, I held you in my arms and slept, at peace in the midst of your sobs, yet annoyed when the hot tears from your eyes dripped upon my lips and I tasted their saltiness and thought about that Sammy and his hideous manuscript. That *he* should strike you! That fool. Even his punctuation was bad.

When we woke up it was morning and we were both nauseated, and your swollen lip was more grotesque than ever, and your black eye was now green. You got up, staggered to the wash-stand and washed your face. I heard you groan. I watched you dress. I felt your kiss on my forehead as you said goodbye, and that nauseated me too. Then you climbed out the window and I heard you stagger up the hillside, the grass swishing and little twigs breaking under your uncertain feet.

I am trying to remember it chronologically. Winter or Spring or Summer, they were days without change. Good for the night, thanks for the darkness, otherwise we would not have known that one day ended and another began. I had 240 pages done and the end was in sight. The rest was a cruise on smooth water. Then off to Hackmuth it would go, tra la, and the agony would begin.

It was about that time that we went to Terminal Island, Camilla and I. A man-made island, that place, a long finger of earth pointing at Catalina. Earth and canneries and the smell of fish, brown houses full of Japanese children, stretches of white sand with wide black pavements running up and down, and the Japanese kids playing football in the streets. She was irritable, she had been drinking too much, and her eyes had that stark old woman's look of a chicken. We parked the car in the broad street and walked a hundred yards to the beach. There were rocks at the water's edge, jagged stones swarming with crabs. The crabs were having a tough time of it, because the sea gulls were after them, and the sea gulls screeched and clawed and fought among themselves. We sat on the sand and watched them, and Camilla said they were so beautiful, those gulls.

"I hate them," I said.

"You!" she said. "You hate everything."

"Look at them," I said. "Why do they pick on those poor crabs? The crabs ain't doing anything. Then why in the hell do they mob them like that?"

"Crabs," she said. "Ugh."

"I hate a sea gull," I said. "They'll eat anything, the deader the better."

"For God's sake shut up for a change. You always spoil everything. What do I care what they eat?"

In the street the little Japanese kids were having a big football game. They were all youngsters under twelve. One of them was a pretty good passer. I turned my back on the sea and watched the game. The good passer had flung another into the arms of one of his teammates. I got interested and sat up.

"Watch the sea," Camilla said. "You're supposed to admire beautiful things, you writer."

"He throws a beautiful pass," I said.

The swelling had gone from her lips, but her eye was still discolored. "I used to come here all the time," she said. "Almost every night."

"With that other writer," I said. "That really great writer, that Sammy the genius."

"He liked it here."

"He's a great writer, alright. That story he wrote over your left eye is a masterpiece."

"He doesn't talk his guts out like you. He knows when to be quiet."

"The stupe."

A fight was brewing between us. I decided to avoid it. I got up and walked toward the kids in the street. She asked where I was going. "I'm going to get in the game," I said. She was outraged. "With them?" she said. "Those Japs?" I plowed through the sand.

132

"Remember what happened the other night!" she said.

I turned around. "What?"

"Remember how you walked home?"

"That suits me," I said. "The bus is safer."

The kids wouldn't let me play because the sides were evenly numbered, but they let me referee for a while. Then the good passer's team got so far ahead that a change was necessary, so I played on the opposite team. Everybody on our team wanted to be quarterback, and great confusion resulted. They made me play center, and I hated it because I was ineligible to receive passes. Finally the captain of our team asked me if I knew how to pass, and he gave me a chance in the tailback spot. I completed the pass. It was fun after that. Camilla left almost immediately. We played until darkness, and they beat us, but it was close. I took the bus back to Los Angeles.

Making resolutions not to see her again was useless. I didn't know from one day to the next. There was the night two days after she left me stranded at Terminal Island. I had been to a picture show. It was after midnight when I went down the old stairway to my room. The door was locked, and from the inside. As I turned the knob I heard her call. "Just a minute. It's me, Arturo."

It was a long minute, five times as long as usual. I could hear her scurrying about within the room. I heard the closet door slam, heard the window being thrown open. I fumbled with the door-knob once more. She opened the door and stood there, breathless, her bosom rising and falling. Her eyes were points of black flame, her cheeks were full of blood, and she seemed alive with intense joy. I stood in a kind of fear at the change, the sudden widening and closing of her lashes, the quick wet smile, the teeth so alive and stringy with bubbled saliva.

I said, "What's the idea?"

She threw her arms around me. She kissed me with a passion I knew was not genuine. She barred my entrance by a flourish of affection. She was hiding something from me, keeping me out of my own room as long as she could. Over her shoulder I looked

133

around. I saw the bed with the mark of a head's indentation upon the pillow. Her coat was flung over the chair, and the dresser was strewn with small combs and bobby pins. That was alright. Everything seemed in order except the two small red mats at the bedside. They had been moved, that was plain to me, because I liked them in their regular place, where my feet could touch them when I got out of bed in the morning.

I pulled her arms away and looked toward the closet door. Suddenly she began to pant excitedly as she backed to the door, standing against it, her arms spread to protect it. "Don't open it, Arturo," she pleaded. "Please!"

"What the hell is all this?" I said.

She shivered. She wet her lips and swallowed, her eyes filled with tears and she both smiled and wept. "I'll tell you sometime," she said. "But please don't go in there now, Arturo. You mustn't. Oh, you mustn't. Please!"

"Who's in there?"

"Nobody," she almost shouted. "Not a soul. That isn't it, Arturo. Nobody's been here. But please! Please don't open it now. Oh please!"

She came toward me, almost stalking, her arms out in an embrace that was yet a protection against my attack on the closet door. She opened her lips and kissed me with peculiar fervor, a passionate coldness, a voluptuous indifference. I didn't like it. Some part of her was betraying some other part, but I could not find it. I sat on the bed and watched her as she stood between me and that closet door. She was trying so hard to conceal a cynical elation. She was like one who is forced to hide his drunkenness, but the elation was there, impossible to conceal.

"You're drunk, Camilla. You shouldn't drink so much."

The eagerness with which she acknowledged that indeed she was drunk made me immediately suspicious. There she stood, nodding her head like a spoiled child, a coy smiling admission, the pouted lips, the look out of downcast eyes. I got up and kissed her. She was drunk, but she was not drunk on whiskey or alcohol because her breath was too sweet for that. I pulled her down on the bed beside me. Her ecstasy swept across her eyes, wave after wave of it, the passionate languor of her arms and fingers searched my throat. She crooned into my hair, her lips against my head.

"If you were only him," she whispered. Suddenly she screamed, a piercing shriek that clawed the walls of the room. "Why can't you be him! Oh Jesus Christ, why can't you?" She began to beat me with her fists, pounding my head with rights and lefts, screaming and scratching in an outburst of madness against the destiny that did not make me her Sammy. I grabbed her wrists, yelled at her to be quiet. I pinned her arms and clamped my hand over her shrieking mouth. She looked out at me with bloated, protruding eyes, struggling for breath. "Not until you promise to keep quiet," I said. She nodded and I let go. I went to the door and listened for footsteps. She lay on the bed, face down, weeping. I tiptoed toward the closet door. Instinct must have warned her. She swung around on the bed, her face soggy with tears, her eyes like crushed grapes.

"You open that door and I'll scream," she said. "I'll scream and scream."

I didn't want that. I shrugged. She resumed her face down position and wept again. In a little while she would cry it off; then I could send her home. But it didn't happen that way. After a half hour she was still crying. I bent over and touched her hair. "What is it you want, Camilla?"

"Him," she sobbed. "I want to go see him."

"Tonight?" I said. "My God, it's a hundred and fifty miles."

She didn't care if it was a thousand miles, a million, she wanted to see him tonight. I told her to go ahead; that was her affair; she had a car, she could drive there in five hours.

"I want you to come with me," she sobbed. "He doesn't like me. He likes you, though."

"Not me," I said. "I'm going to bed."

She pleaded with me. She fell on her knees before me, clung to my legs and looked up at me. She loved him so much, surely a great writer like myself understood what it was to love like that; surely I knew why she couldn't go out there alone; and she touched the injured eye. Sammy wouldn't drive her off if I were to come with her. He'd be grateful that she had brought me, and then Sammy and I could talk, because there was so much I could show him about writing, and he would be so grateful to me, and to her. I looked down at her, gritted my teeth, and tried to resist her arguments; but when she put it that way it was too much for me, and when I agreed to go I was crying with her. I helped her to her feet, dried her eyes, smoothed the hair from her face, and felt responsible for her. We tiptoed up the stairs and through the lobby to the street, where her car was parked.

We drove south and slightly east, each of us taking a turn at the wheel. By dawn we were in a land of grey desolation, of cactus and sagebrush and Joshua trees, a desert where the sand was scarce and the whole vast plain was pimpled with tumbled rocks and scarred by stumpy little hills. Then we turned off the main highway and entered a wagon trail clogged with boulders and rarely used. The road rose and fell to the rhythm of the listless hills. It was daylight when we came to a region of canyons and steep gulches, twenty miles in the interior of the Mojave Desert. There below us was where Sammy lived, and Camilla pointed to a squat adobe shack planted at the bottom of three sharp hills. It was at the very edge of a sandy plain. To the east the plain spread away infinitely.

We were both tired, hammered to exhaustion by the bouncing Ford. It was very cold at that hour. We had to park two hundred yards from the house and take a stony path to its door. I led the way. At the door I paused. Inside I could hear a man snoring heavily. Camilla hung back, her arms folded against the sharp cold. I knocked and got a groan in response. I knocked again, and then I heard Sammy's voice. "If that's you, you little Spick, I'll kick your goddamn teeth out."

He opened the door and I saw a face clutched in the persistent fingers of sleep, the eyes grey and dazed, the hair in ruins across his forehead. "Hello, Sammy."

"Oh," he said. "I thought it was her."

"She's here," I said.

"Tell her to screw outa' here. I don't want her around."

She had retreated to a place against the wall of the hut, and I looked at her and saw her smiling away her embarrassment. The three of us were very cold, our jaws chattering. Sammy opened the door wider. "You can come in," he said. "But not her."

I stepped inside. It was almost pitch dark, smelling of old underwear and the sleep of a sick body. A feeble light came from a crack in the window covered by a slice of sacking. Before I could stop him, Sammy had bolted the door.

He stood in long underwear. The floor was of dirt, dry and sandy and cold. He yanked the sacking from the window and the early light tumbled through. Vapors spilled from our mouths in the cold air. "Let her in, Sammy," I said. "What the hell."

"Not that bitch," he said.

He stood in long underwear, the knees and elbows capped with the blackness of dirt. He was tall, gaunt, a cadaver of a man, tanned almost to blackness. He padded across the hut to a coal stove and began making a fire. His voice changed and became soft when he spoke. "Wrote another story last week," he said. "Think I got a good one this time. Like you to see it."

"Sure," I said. "But hell, Sammy. She's a friend of mine."

"Bah," he said. "She's no good. Crazy as hell. Cause you nothing but trouble."

"Let her in anyway. It's cold out there."

He opened the door and pushed his head out.

"Hey, you!"

I heard the girl sob, heard her try to compose herself. "Yes, Sammy."

"Don't stand out there like a fool," he said. "You coming in or ain't you?"

She entered like a frightened deer while he went back to the stove. "Thought I told you I didn't want you hanging around here no more," he said.

"I brought him," she said. "Arturo. He wanted to talk to you about writing. Didn't you, Arturo?"

"That's right."

She was like a stranger to me. All the fight and glory of her was

137

drained like blood from her veins. She stood off by herself, a creature without spirit or will, her shoulder blades humped, her head drooping as though too heavy for her neck.

"You," Sammy said to her. "Go get some wood, you."

"I'll go," I said.

"Let her go," he said. "She knows where it is."

I watched her slink out the door. In a while she came back, her arms loaded. She dumped the sticks into a box beside the stove, and without speaking she fed the flames, a stick at a time. Sammy sat on a box across the room, pulling on his socks. He talked incessantly about his stories, a continuous flow of chatter. Camilla stood dismally beside the stove.

"You," he said. "Make some coffee."

She did as she was told, serving us coffee out of tin cups. Sammy, fresh from sleep, was full of enthusiasm and curiosity. We sat at the fire, and I was tired and sleepy, and the hot fire toyed with my heavy lids. Behind us and all around us, Camilla worked. She swept the place out, made up the bed, washed dishes, hung up stray garments and kept up an incessant activity. The more Sammy talked, the more cordial and personal he became. He was interested in the financial side of writing more than in writing itself. How much did this magazine pay, and how much did that one pay, and he was convinced that only by favoritism were stories sold. You had to have a cousin or a brother or somebody like that in an editor's office before they took one of your stories. It was useless to try to dissuade him, and I didn't try, because I knew that his kind of rationalizing was necessary in view of his sheer inability to write well.

Camilla cooked breakfast for us, and we ate from plates on our laps. The fare was fried corn meal and bacon and eggs. Sammy ate with the peculiar robustness of unhealthy people. After the meal, Camilla gathered the tin plates and washed them. Then she had her own breakfast, seated in a far corner, quiet except for the sound of her fork against the tin plate. All that long morning Sammy talked. Sammy really didn't need any advice about writing. Vaguely through the fog of semi-slumber I heard him telling me how it should and shouldn't be done. But I was so tired. I begged to be excused. He led me outside to an arbor of palm branches. Now the air was warm and the sun was high. I lay in the hammock and fell asleep, and the last thing I remember was the sight of Camilla bent over a wash tub filled with dark water and several pairs of underwear and overalls.

Six hours later she woke me to tell me that it was two o'clock, and that we had to start back. She was due at the Columbia Buffet at seven. I asked her if she had slept. She shook her head negatively. Her face was a manuscript of misery and exhaustion. I got off the hammock and stood up in the hot desert air. My clothes were soaked in perspiration, but I was rested and refreshed.

"Where's the genius?" I said.

She nodded toward the hut. I walked toward the door, ducking under a long heavy clothesline sagging with clean, dry garments. "You did all of that?" I asked. She smiled. "It was fun."

Deep snores came from the hut. I peeked inside. On the bunk lay Sammy, half naked, his mouth wide open, his arms and legs spread apart. I tiptoed away. "Now's our chance," I said. "Let's go."

She entered the hut and quietly walked to where Sammy lay. From the door I watched her lean over him, study his face and body. Then she bent down, her face near his, as if to kiss him. At that moment he awoke and their eyes met. He said: "Get out of here."

She turned and walked out. We drove back to Los Angeles in complete silence. Even when she let me out at the Alta Loma Hotel, even then we did not speak, but she smiled her thanks and I smiled my sympathy, and she drove away. Already it was dark, a smudge of the pink sunset fading in the west. I went down to my room, yawned, and threw myself on the bed. Lying there I suddenly remembered the clothes closet. I got up and opened the closet door. Everything seemed as it should, my suits hanging from hooks, my suitcases on the top shelf. But there was no light in the closet. I struck a match and looked down at the floor. In the corner was a burned matchstick and a score of grains of brown stuff, like coarsely ground coffee. I pressed my finger into the stuff and then tasted it on the end of my tongue. I knew what that was: it was marijuana. I was sure of it, because Benny Cohen had once showed me the stuff to warn me against it. So that was why she had been in here. You had to have an air-tight room to smoke marijuana. That explained why the two rugs had been moved: she had used them to cover the crack under the door.

Camilla was a hophead. I sniffed the closet air, put my nostrils against the garments hanging there. The smell was that of burned cornsilk. Camilla, the hophead.

It was none of my business, but she was Camilla; she had tricked me and scorned me, and she loved somebody else, but she *was* so beautiful and I needed her so, and I decided to make it my business. I was waiting in her car at eleven that night.

"So you're a hophead," I said.

"Once in a while," she said. "When I'm tired."

"You cut it out," I said.

"It's not a habit," she said.

"Cut it out anyway."

She shrugged. "It doesn't bother me."

"Promise me you'll quit."

She made a cross over her heart. "Cross my heart and hope to die," but she was talking to Arturo now, and not to Sammy. I knew she would not keep the promise. She started the car and drove down Broadway to Eighth, then south toward Central Avenue. "Where we going?" I said.

"Wait and see."

We drove into the Los Angeles Black Belt, Central Avenue, night clubs, abandoned apartment houses, broken-down business houses, the forlorn street of poverty for the Negro and swank for the whites. We stopped under the marquee of a night spot called the Club Cuba. Camilla knew the doorman, a giant in a blue uniform with gold buttons. "Business," she said. He grinned, signaled someone to take his place, and jumped on the running board. It was done like a routine procedure, as though it had been done before.

She drove around the corner and continued for two streets, until we came to an alley. She turned down the alley, switched off the lights and steered carefully into pitch blackness. We came to some kind of opening and killed the engine. The big Negro jumped off the running board and snapped on a flashlight, motioning us to follow. "May I ask just what the hell this is all about?" I said.

We entered a door. The Negro took the lead. He held Camilla's hand, and she held mine. We walked down a long corridor. It was carpetless, a hardwood floor. Far away like frightened birds, the echo of our feet floated through the upper floors. We climbed three flights of stairs and proceeded the length of another hall. At the end was a door. The Negro opened it. Inside was complete darkness. We entered. The room reeked with smoke that could not be seen, and yet it burned like an eyewash. The smoke choked my throat, leaped for my nostrils. In the darkness I swallowed for breath. Then the Negro flashed on his light.

The beam traveled around the room, a small room. Everywhere were bodies, the bodies of Negroes, men and women, perhaps a score of them, lying on the floor and across a bed that was only a mattress on springs. I could see their eyes, wide and grey and oyster-like as the flashlight hit them, and gradually I accustomed myself to the burning smoke and saw tiny red points of light everywhere, for they were all smoking marijuana, quietly in the darkness, and the pungency stabbed my lungs. The big Negro cleared the bed of its occupants, flung them like so many sacks of grain to the floor, and the flash spot revealed him digging something from a slot in the mattress. It was a Prince Albert tobacco can. He opened the door, and we followed him down the stairs and through the same darkness to the car. He handed the can to Camilla, and she gave him two dollars. We drove him back to his doorman's job, and then we continued down Central Avenue to metropolitan Los Angeles.

I was speechless. We drove to her place on Temple Street. It was a sick building, a frame place diseased and dying from the sun. She lived in an apartment. There was a Murphy bed, a radio, and dirty blue overstuffed furniture. The carpeted floor was littered with crumbs and dirt, and in the corner, sprawled out like one naked, lay a movie magazine. There were kewpie dolls standing about, souvenirs of gaudy nights at beach resorts. There was a bicycle in the corner, the flat tires attesting to long disuse. There was a fishing pole in one corner with tangled hooks and line, and there was a shotgun in the other corner, dusty. There was a baseball bat under the divan, and there was a bible lodged between the cushions of the overstuffed chair. The bed was down, and the sheets were not clean. There was a reproduction of the Blue Boy on one wall and a print of an Indian Brave saluting the sky on another.

I walked into the kitchen, smelled the garbage in the sink, saw the greasy frying pans on the stove. I opened the Frigidaire and it was empty save for a can of condensed milk and a cube of butter. The icebox door would not close, and that seemed as it should be. I looked into the closet behind the Murphy bed and there were lots of clothes and lots of clothes-hooks, but all the clothes were on the floor, except a straw hat, and that hung alone, ridiculous up there by itself.

So this was where she lived! I smelled it, touched it with my fingers, walked through it with my feet. It was as I had imagined. This was her home. Blindfolded I could have acknowledged the place, for her odor possessed it, her fevered, lost existence proclaimed it as part of a hopeless scheme. An apartment on Temple Street, an apartment in Los Angeles. She belonged to the rolling hills, the wide deserts, the high mountains, she would ruin any apartment, she would lay havoc upon any such little prison as this. It was so, ever in my imagination, ever a part of my scheming and thinking about her. This was her home, her ruin, her scattered dream.

She threw off her coat and flung herself on the divan. I watched her stare dismally at the ugly carpet. Sitting in the overstuffed chair, I puffed a cigaret and let my eyes wander the profile of her curved back and hips. The dark corridor of that Central Avenue Hotel, the sinister Negro, the black room and the hopheads, and now the girl who loved a man who hated her. It was all of the same cloth, perverse, drugged in fascinating ugliness. Midnight on

Temple Street, a can of marijuana between us. She lay there, her long fingers dangling to the carpet, waiting, listless, tired.

"Have you ever tried it?" she asked.

"Not me," I said.

"Once won't hurt you."

"Not me."

She sat up, fumbled for the can of marijuana in her purse. She drew out a packet of cigaret papers. She poured a paperful, rolled it, licked it, pinched the ends, and handed it to me. I took it, and yet I said, "Not me."

She rolled one for herself. Then she arose and closed the windows, clamped them tightly by their latches. She dragged a blanket off the bed and laid it against the crack of the door. She looked around carefully. She looked at me. She smiled. "Everybody acts different," she said. "Maybe you'll feel sad, and cry."

"Not me," I said.

She lit hers, held the match for mine.

"I shouldn't be doing this," I said.

"Inhale," she said. "Then hold it. Hold it a long time. Until it hurts. Then let it out."

"This is bad business," I said.

I inhaled it. I held it. I held it a long time, until it hurt. Then I let it out. She lay back against the divan and did the same thing. "Sometimes it takes two of them," she said.

"It won't affect me," I said.

We smoked them down until they burned our fingertips. Then I rolled two more. In the middle of the second it began to come, the floating, the wafting away from the earth, the joy and triumph of a man over space, the extraordinary sense of power. I laughed and inhaled again. She lay there, the cold languor of the night before upon her face, the cynical passion. But I was beyond the room, beyond the limits of my flesh, floating in a land of bright moons and blinking stars. I was invincible. I was not myself, I had never been that fellow with his grim happiness, his strange bravery. A lamp on the table beside me, and I picked it up and looked at it, and dropped it to the floor. It broke into many pieces. I laughed. She heard the noise, saw the ruin, and laughed too.

"What's funny?" I said.

She laughed again. I got up, crossed the room, and took her in my arms. They felt terribly strong and she panted at their crush and desire.

I watched her stand and take off her clothes, and somewhere out of an earthly past I remembered having seen that face of hers before, that obedience and fear, and I remembered a hut and Sammy telling her to go out and get some wood. It was as I knew it was bound to be sooner or later. She crept into my arms and I laughed at her tears.

When it was all gone, the dream of floating toward bursting stars, and the flesh returned to hold my blood in its prosaic channels, when the room returned, the dirty sordid room, the vacant meaningless ceiling, the weary wasted world, I felt nothing but the old sense of guilt, the sense of crime and violation, the sin of destruction. I sat beside her as she lay on the divan. I stared at the carpet. I saw the pieces of glass from the broken lamp. And when I got up to walk across the room, I felt the pain, the sharp agony of the flesh of my feet torn by my own weight. It hurt with a deserving pain. My feet were cut when I put on my shoes and walked out of that apartment and into the bright astonishment of the night. Limping, I walked the long road to my room. I thought I would never see Camilla Lopez again.

Chapter Seventeen

But big events were coming, and I had no one to whom I could speak of them. There was the day I finished the story of Vera Rivken, the breezy days of rewriting it, just coasting along, Hackmuth, a few more days now and you'll see something great. Then the revision was finished and I sent it away, and then the waiting, the hoping. I prayed once more. I went to mass and Holy Communion. I made a novena. I lit candles at the Blessed Virgin's altar. I prayed for a miracle.

The miracle happened. It happened like this: I was standing at the window in my room, watching a bug crawling along the sill. It was three-fifteen on a Thursday afternoon. There was a knock on my door. I opened the door, and there he stood, a telegraph boy. I signed for the telegram, sat on the bed, and wondered if the wine had finally got the Old Man's heart. The telegram said: your book accepted mailing contract today. Hackmuth. That was all. I let the paper float to the carpet. I just sat there. Then I got down on the floor and began kissing the telegram. I crawled under the bed and just lay there. I did not need the sunshine anymore. Nor the earth, nor heaven. I just lay there, happy to die. Nothing else could happen to me. My life was over.

Was the contract coming via air mail? I paced the floor those next days. I read the papers. Air mail was too impractical, too dangerous. Down with the air mail. Every day planes were falling, covering the earth with wreckage, killing pilots: it was too damned unsafe, a pioneering venture, and where the hell was my contract? I called the post office. How were flying conditions over the Sierras? Good. All planes accounted for? Good. No wrecks? Then where was my contract? I spent a long time practicing my signature. I decided to use my middle name, the whole thing Arturo Dominic Bandini, A. D. Bandini, Arturo D. Bandini, A. Dominic Bandini.

The contract came Monday morning, first class mail. With it was a check for five hundred dollars. My God, five hundred dollars! I was one of the Morgans. I could retire for life.

War in Europe, a speech by Hitler, trouble in Poland, these were the topics of the day. What piffle! You warmongers, you old folks in the lobby of the Alta Loma Hotel, here is the news, here: this little paper with all the fancy legal writing, my book! To hell with that Hitler, this is more important than Hitler, this is about my book. It won't shake the world, it won't kill a soul, it won't fire a gun, ah, but you'll remember it to the day you die, you'll lie there breathing your last, and you'll smile as you remember the book. The story of Vera Rivken, a slice out of life.

They weren't interested. They preferred the war in Europe, the funny pictures, and Louella Parsons, the tragic people, the poor people. I just sat in that hotel lobby and shook my head sadly.

Someone had to know, and that was Camilla. For three weeks I had not seen her, not since the marijuana on Temple Street. But she was not at the saloon. Another girl had her place. I asked for Camilla. The other girl wouldn't talk. Suddenly the Columbia Buffet was like a tomb. I asked the fat bartender. Camilla had not been there for two weeks. Was she fired? He couldn't say. Was she sick? He didn't know. He wouldn't talk either.

I could afford a taxicab. I could afford twenty cabs, riding them day and night. I took one cab and rode to Camilla's place on Temple Street. I knocked on her door and got no answer. I tried the door. It opened, darkness inside, and I switched on the light. She lay there in the Murphy bed. Her face was the face of an old rose pressed and dried in a book, yellowish, with only the eyes to prove there was life in it. The room stank. The blinds were down, the door opened with difficulty until I kicked away the rug against the crack. She gasped when she saw me. She was happy to see me. "Arturo," she said. "Oh, Arturo!"

I didn't speak of the book or the contract. Who cares about a novel, another goddamn novel? That sting in my eyes, it was for her, it was my eyes remembering a wild lean girl running in the moonlight on the beach, a beautiful girl who danced with a beer-tray in her round arms. She lay there now, broken, brown cigaret butts overflowing a saucer beside her. She had quit. She wanted to die. Those were her words. "I don't care," she said.

"You gotta eat," I said, because her face was only a skull with yellow skin stretched tightly over it. I sat on the bed and held her fingers, conscious of bones, surprised that they were such small bones, she who had been so straight and round and tall. "You're hungry," I said. But she didn't want food. "Eat anyway," I said.

I went out and started buying. It was a few doors down the street, a small grocery store. I ordered whole sections of the place. Gimme all of those, and all of these, gimme this and gimme that. Milk, bread, canned juices, fruit, butter, vegetables, meat, potatoes. It took three trips to carry it all up to her place. When it was all piled there in the kitchen I looked at the stuff and scratched my head, wondering what to feed her.

"I don't want anything," she said.

Milk. I washed a glass and poured it full. She sat up, her pink nightgown torn at the shoulder, ripping all the more as she moved to sit up. She held her nose and drank it, three swallows, and she gasped and lay back, horrified, nauseated.

"Fruit juice," I said. "Grape juice. It's sweeter, tastes better." I opened a bottle, poured a glassful, and held it out to her. She gulped it down, lay back and panted. Then she put her head over the side of the bed and vomited. I cleaned it up. I cleaned the apartment. I washed the dishes and scrubbed the sink. I washed her face. I hurried downstairs, grabbed a cab, and rode all over town looking for a place to buy her a clean nightgown. I bought some candy too, and a stack of picture magazines, *Look*, *Pic*, *See*, *Sic*, *Sac*, *Whack*, and all of them—something to distract her, to put her at ease.

When I got back the door was locked. I knew what that meant. I hammered it with my fists and kicked it with my heels. The din filled the whole building. The doors of other apartments opened in the hall, and heads came out. From downstairs a woman came in an old bathrobe. She was the landlady; I could spot a landlady instantly. She stood at the head of the stairs, afraid to come closer.

147

"What do you want?" she said.

"It's locked," I said. "I have to get inside."

"You leave that girl alone," she said. "I know your kind. You leave that poor girl alone or I'll call the police."

"I'm her friend," I said.

From inside came the elated, hysterical laughter of Camilla, the giddy shriek of denial. "He's not my friend! I don't want him around!" Then her laughter once more, high and frightened and birdlike, trapped in the room. Now the hall was full of people in a state of semi-undress. The atmosphere was nasty, ominous. Two men in shirt sleeves appeared at the other end of the hall. The big one with a cigar hitched up his pants and said, "Let's throw the guy out of here." I started moving then, retreating from them walking fast, past the despicable sneer of the landlady and down the stairs to the lower hall. Once in the street I started running. On the corner of Broadway and Temple I saw a cab parked. I got in and told the driver to just keep moving.

No, it was none of my business. But I could remember, the black cluster of her hair, the wild depth of her eyes, the jolt in the pit of my stomach in the first days I knew her. I stayed away from the place for two days, and then I couldn't bear it: I wanted to help her. I wanted to get her away from that curtained trap, send her somewhere to the south, down by the sea. I could do it. I had a pile of money. I thought of Sammy, but he loathed her too deeply. If she could only get out of town, that would help a lot. I decided to try once more.

It was about noon. It was very hot, too hot in the hotel room. It was the heat that made me do it, the sticky ennui, the dust over the earth, the hot blasts from the Mojave. I went to the rear of the Temple Street apartment. There was a wooden stairway leading to the second floor. On such a day as this, her door would be open, to cool the place by cross ventilation from the window.

I was right. The door was open, but she was not there. Her stuff was piled in the middle of the room, boxes and suitcases with garments squirming from them. The bed was down, the naked mattress showing the sheets gone. The place was stripped of life. Then

I caught the odor of disinfectant. The room had been fumigated. I took the stairs three at a time to the landlady's door.

"You!" she said, opening the door. "You!" and she slammed it shut. I stood outside and pleaded with her. "I'm her friend," I said. "I swear to God. I want to help her. You got to believe me."

"Go away or I'll call the police."

"She was sick," I said. "She needed help. I want to do something for her. You've got to believe me."

The door opened. The woman stood looking straight into my eyes. She was of medium height, stout, her face hardened and without emotion. She said: "Come in."

I stepped into a drab room, ornate and weird, cluttered with fantastic gadgets, a piano littered with heavy photographs, wild-colored shawls, fancy lamps and vases. She asked me to sit down, but I didn't.

"That girl's gone," she said. "She's gone crazy. I had to do it."

"Where is she? What happened?"

"I had to do it. She was a nice girl too."

She had been forced to call the police—that was her story. That had happened the night after I was there. Camilla had gone wild, throwing dishes, dumping furniture out of the window, screaming and kicking the walls, slashing the curtains with a knife. The landlady had called the police. The police had come, broken down the door, and seized her. But the police had refused to take her away. They had held her, quieted her, until an ambulance arrived. Wailing and struggling, she had been led away. That was all, except that Camilla owed three weeks' rent and had done irreparable damage to the furniture and apartment. The landlady mentioned a figure, and I paid her the money. She handed me a receipt and smiled her greasy hypocrisy. "I knew you were a good boy," she said. "I knew it from the moment I first laid eyes on you. But you just can't trust strangers in this town."

I took the street car to the County Hospital. The nurse in the reception room checked a card file when I mentioned the name of Camilla Lopez. "She's here," the nurse said. "But she can't have visitors."

"How is she?"

"I can't answer that."

"When can I see her?"

Visiting day was Wednesday. I had to wait four more days. I walked out of the huge hospital and around the grounds. I looked up at the windows and wandered through the grounds. Then I took the street car back to Hill Street and Bunker Hill. Four days to wait. I exhausted them playing pin games and slot machines. Luck was against me. I lost a lot of money, but I killed a lot of time. Tuesday afternoon I walked downtown and started buying things for Camilla. I bought a portable radio, a box of candy, a dressing gown, and a lot of face creams and such things. Then I went to a flower shop and ordered two dozen camellias. I was loaded down when I got to the hospital Wednesday afternoon. The camellias had wilted overnight because I didn't think about putting them in water. Sweat poured from my face as I climbed the hospital steps. I knew my freckles were in bloom, I could almost feel them popping out of my face.

The same nurse was at the reception desk. I unloaded the gifts into a chair and asked to see Camilla Lopez. The nurse checked the file card. "Miss Lopez isn't here anymore," she said. "She's been transferred." I was so hot and so tired. "Where is she?" I said. I groaned when she said she couldn't answer that. "I'm her friend," I told the nurse. "I want to help her."

"I'm sorry," the nurse said.

"Who'll tell me?"

Yes, who'll tell me? I went all over the hospital, up one floor and down the other. I saw doctors and assistant doctors, I saw nurses, and assistant nurses, I waited in lobbies and halls, but nobody would tell me anything. They all reached for the little card file, and they all said the same thing: she had been transferred. But she wasn't dead. They all denied that, coming quickly to the point; no, she wasn't dead: they had taken her elsewhere. It was useless. I walked out the front door and into the blinding sunlight to the street car line. Boarding the car, I remembered the gifts. They were back there somewhere; I couldn't even remember which waiting room. I didn't care. Disconsolate, I rode back to Bunker Hill.

If she had been transferred, it meant another State or County institution, because she had no money. Money. I had the money. I had three pocketfuls of money, and more at home in my other pants. I could get it all together and bring it to them, but they wouldn't even tell me what had happened to her. What was money for? I was going to spend it anyway, and those halls, those etherized halls, those low-voiced enigmatic doctors, those quiet, reticent nurses, they baffled me. I got off the street car in a daze. Halfway up the stairs of Bunker Hill I sat down in a doorway and looked down at the city below me in the nebulous, dusty haze of the late afternoon. The heat rose out of the haze and my nostrils breathed it. Over the city spread a white murkiness like fog. But it was not the fog: it was the desert heat, the great blasts from the Mojave and Santa Ana, the pale white fingers of the wasteland, ever reaching out to claim its captured child.

The next day I found out what they had done to Camilla. From a drugstore downtown I called long distance and got the switchboard at County Institute for the Insane at Del Maria. I asked the switchboard girl for the name of the doctor in charge there. "Doctor Danielson," she said.

"Give me his office."

She plugged the board and another woman's voice came through the wire. "Dr. Danielson's office."

"This is Dr. Jones," I said. "Let me speak to Dr. Danielson. This is urgent."

"One moment please."

Then a man's voice. "Danielson speaking."

"Hello, Doctor," I said. "This is Dr. Jones, Edmond Jones, Los Angeles. You have a transfer there from the County Hospital, a Miss Camilla Lopez. How is she?"

"We can't say," Danielson said. "She's still under observation. Did you say Edmond Jones?"

I hung up. At least I knew where she was. Knowing that was one thing; trying to see her was another. It was out of the question. I talked to people who knew. You had to be a relative of an inmate, and you had to prove it. You had to write for an appointment, and you came after they had investigated. You couldn't write the inmates a letter, and you couldn't send gifts. I didn't go out to Del Maria. I was satisfied that I had done my best. She was insane, and it was none of my business. Besides, she loved Sammy.

The days passed, the winter rains began. Late October, and the proofs of my book arrived. I bought a car, a 1929 Ford. It had no top, but it sped like the wind, and with the coming of dry days I took long rides along the blue coastline, up to Ventura, up to Santa Barbara, down to San Clemente, down to San Diego, following the white line of the pavement, under the staring stars, my feet on the dashboard, my head full of plans for another book, one night and then another, all of them together spelling dream days I had never known, serene days I feared to question. I prowled the city with my Ford: I found mysterious alleys, lonely trees, rotting old houses out of a vanished past. Day and night I lived in my Ford, pausing only long enough to order a hamburger and a cup of coffee at strange roadside cafes. This was the life for a man, to wander and stop and then go on, ever following the white line along the rambling coast, a time to relax at the wheel, light another cigaret, and grope stupidly for the meanings in that perplexing desert sky.

One night I came upon the place at Santa Monica where Camilla and I had gone swimming in those first days. I stopped and watched the foamy breakers and the mysterious mist. I remembered the girl running through the foaming thunder, reveling in the wild freedom of that night. Oh, that Camilla, that girl!

There was that night in the middle of November, when I was walking down Spring Street, poking around in the secondhand bookstores. The Columbia Buffet was only a block away. Just for the devil of it, I said, for old time's sake, and I walked up to the bar and ordered a beer. I was an old-timer now. I could look around sneeringly and remember when this was really a wonderful place. But not any more. Nobody knew me, neither the new barmaid with her jaw full of gum, nor the two female musicians still grinding out *Tales from the Vienna Woods* on a violin and a piano.

And yet the fat bartender did remember me. Steve, or Vince, or Vinnie, or whatever his name. "Ain't seen you in a long time," he said.

"Not since Camilla," I said.

He clucked his tongue. "Too bad," he said. "Nice kid too." That was all. I drank another beer, then a third. He gave me the fourth, and then I bought for the two of us on the next round. An hour passed in that fashion. He stood before me, reached into his pocket, and drew out a newspaper clipping. "I suppose you already seen this," he said. I picked it up. It was no more than six lines, and a two line headline from the bottom of an inside page:

> Local police today were on the lookout
> for Camilla Lopez, 22, of Los Angeles,
> whose disappearance from the Del Maria
> institution was discovered by authorities
> last night.

The clipping was a week old. I left my beer and hurried out of there and up the hill to my room. Something told me she was coming there. I could feel her desire to return to my room. Pulling up a chair, I sat with my feet in the window, the lights on, smoking and waiting. Deeply I felt she would come, convinced there was no one else to whom she could turn. But she did not come. I went to bed, leaving the lights on. Most of the next day and all through the following night I stayed in my room, waiting for the plink of pebbles against my window. After the third night the conviction that she was coming began to wane. No, she would not come here. She would flee to Sammy, to her true love. The last person of whom she would think would be Arturo Bandini. That suited me just fine. After all, I was a novelist now, and something of a short story writer too, even if I did say so myself.

The next morning I got the first of her collect telegrams. It was a request for money to be wired to Rita Gomez, care of Western Union, San Francisco. She had signed the wire "Rita" but the identity was obvious. I wired her twenty and told her to come south as far as Santa Barbara, where I would meet her. She wired this answer: "Would rather go north thanks sorry Rita."

The second wire came from Fresno. It was another request for money, to be sent to Rita Gomez, care of Postal Telegraph. That was two days after the first wire. I walked downtown and wired her fifteen. For a long time I sat in the telegraph office composing a message to go with the money, but I couldn't make up my mind. I finally gave up and sent the money alone. Nothing I said made any difference to Camilla Lopez. But one thing was certain. I vowed it on the way back to the hotel: she would get no more money out of me. I had to be careful from now on.

Her third wire arrived Sunday night, the same kind of message, this time from Bakersfield. I clung to my resolution for two hours. Then I pictured her wandering around, penniless, probably caught in the rain. I sent her fifty, with a message to buy some clothes and keep out of the rain.

Chapter Eighteen

Three nights later I came home from a ride to find my hotel door locked from the inside. I knew what that meant. I knocked but got no answer. I called her name. I hurried down the hall to the back door and ran up the hillside to the level of my window. I wanted to catch her redhanded. The window was down and so was the curtain on the inside, but there was an opening in the curtain and I could see into the room. It was lighted by a desk lamp and I could see all of it, but I couldn't see her anywhere. The clothes closet door was locked, and I knew she was in there. I pried the window open. I pushed the glass quietly and slipped inside. The bed rugs were not on the floor. On tiptoe I walked toward the closet door. I could hear her moving inside the closet, as though she were sitting on the floor. Faintly I caught the cubeb-like smell of marijuana.

I reached for the knob of the closet door, and all at once I didn't want to catch her at it. The shock would be as bad for me as for her. Then I remembered something that had happened to me when I was a little boy. It was a closet like that one, and my mother had opened it suddenly. I remembered that terror of being discovered, and I tiptoed from the closet door and sat in the chair at my desk. After five minutes I couldn't stay in the room. I didn't want her to know. I crept out of the window, closed it, and returned to the back door of the hotel. I took my time. When I thought it must be over, I walked loudly and briskly toward the door of my room and barged in.

She lay on the bed, a thin hand shielding her eyes. "Camilla!" I said. "You here!" She rose and looked at me with delirious black eyes, black and wanton and in a dream, her neck stretched and defining the bulging cords at her throat. She had nothing to say with her lips, but the ghastly cast of her face, the teeth too white and too big now, the frightened smile, these spoke too loudly of the horror shrouding her days and nights. I bit into my jaws to keep from crying. As I walked toward the bed, she pulled up her knees, slipping into a crouched frightened position, as though she expected me to strike her.

"Take it easy," I said. "You'll be alright. You look swell."

"Thanks for the money," she said, and it was the same voice, deep, yet nasal. She had bought new clothes. They were cheap and garish: an imitiation silk dress of bright yellow with a black velvet belt; blue and yellow shoes and ankle-length stockings with greens and reds forming the tops. Her nails were manicured, polished a blood red, and around her wrists were green and yellow beads. All of this was set against the ash-yellow of her bloodless face and throat. She had always looked her best in the plain white smock she wore at work. I didn't ask any questions. Everything I wanted to know was written in tortured phrases across the desolation of her face. It didn't look like insanity to me. It looked like fear, the terrible fear screaming from her big hungered eyes, alert now from the drug.

She couldn't stay in Los Angeles. She needed rest, a chance to eat and sleep, drink a lot of milk and take long walks. All at once I was full of plans. Laguna Beach! That was the place for her. It was winter now, and we could get a place cheap. I could take care of her and get started on another book. I had an idea for a new book. We didn't have to be married, brother and sister was alright with me. We could go swimming and take long walks along the Balboa shore. We could sit by the fireplace when the fog was heavy. We could sleep under deep blankets when the wind roared off the sea. That was the basic idea: but I elaborated, I poured it into her ears like words from a dream book, and her face brightened, and she cried.

"And a dog!" I said. "I'll get you a little dog. A little pup. A Scottie. And we'll call him Willie."

She clapped her hands. "Oh Willie!" she said. "Here, Willie! Here, Willie!"

"And a cat," I said. "A Siamese cat. We'll call him Chang. A big cat with golden eyes."

She shivered and covered her face with her hands. "No," she said. "I hate cats."

"Okay. No cats. I hate them too."

She was dreaming it all, filling in a picture with her own brush, the elation like bright glass in her eyes. "A horse too," she said. "After you make a lot of money we'll both have a horse."

"I'll make millions," I said.

I undressed and got into bed. She slept badly, jerking awake suddenly, moaning and mumbling in her sleep. Sometime during the night she sat up, turned on the light, and smoked a cigaret. I lay with my eyes closed, trying to sleep. Soon she got up, pulled my bathrobe around her, and found her purse on the desk. It was a white oil-cloth purse, bulging with stuff. I heard her shuffle down the hall to the lavatory in my slippers. She was gone ten minutes. When she returned a calm had come over her. She believed me asleep, kissed me on the temple. I caught the smell of the marijuana. The rest of the night she slept heavily, her face bathed in peace.

At eight the next morning we climbed out the hotel window and went down the hillside to the back of the hotel, where my Ford was parked. She was wretched, her face bitter and sleepless. I drove through town and out Crenshaw, and from there to Long Beach Boulevard. She sat scowling, her head down, the cold wind of the morning combing her hair. In Maywood we stopped at a roadside cafe for breakfast. I had sausage and eggs, fruit juice and coffee. She refused everything but black coffee. After the first swallow she lit a cigaret. I wanted to examine her purse, for I knew it contained marijuana, but she clung to it like life itself. We each had another cup of coffee, and then we drove on. She felt better, but her mood was still dark. I didn't talk.

A couple of miles outside of Long Beach we came upon a dog farm. I drove in and we got out. We were in a yard of palm and eucalyptus trees. From all points a dozen dogs charged us, barking joyously. The dogs loved her, sensed her instantly as their friend, and for the first time that morning she smiled. They were collies, police dogs, and terriers. She dropped to her knees to embrace them, and they overwhelmed her with their yelps and their big pink tongues. She took a terrier in her arms and swayed him like an infant, crooning her affection. Her face was bright again, full of color, the face of the old Camilla.

The kennel owner emerged from his back porch. He was an old man with a short white beard, and he limped and carried a cane. The dogs paid little attention to me. They came up, sniffed my shoes and legs, and turned away sharply, with considerable contempt. It was not that they disliked me; they preferred Camilla with her lavishing emotion and her strange dog-talk. I told the old man we wanted some kind of a pup, and he asked what kind. It was up to Camilla, but she couldn't make up her mind. We saw several litters. They were all touchingly infantile, furry little balls of irresistible tenderness. Finally we came upon the dog she wanted: he was pure white, a collie. He was not quite six weeks old, and he was so fat he could scarcely walk. Camilla put him down, and he staggered through her legs, walked a few feet, sat down, and promptly fell asleep. More than any other, she wanted that pup.

I swallowed when the old man said. "Twenty-five dollars," but we took the pup along, with his papers, with his pure white mother following us to the car, barking as if to tell us to be very careful how we raised him. As we drove away I looked over my shoulder. In the driveway sat the white mother, her beautiful ears perked, her head cocked sidewise, watching us as we disappeared into the main highway.

"Willie," I said. "His name's Willie."

The dog lay in her lap, whimpering.

"No," she said. "It's Snow White."

"That's a girl's name," I said.

"I don't care."

I pulled over to the side of the road. "I care," I said "Either you change his name to something else, or he goes back."

"Alright," she admitted. "His name's Willie."

I felt better. We had not fought about it. Willie was already helping her. She was almost docile, ready to be reasonable. Her restlessness was gone, and a softness curved her lips. Willie was sound asleep in her lap, but he sucked her little finger. South of Long Beach we stopped at a drugstore and bought a bottle with a nipple, and a bottle of milk. Willie's eyes opened when she put the nipple to his mouth. He fell to his task like a fiend. Camilla lifted her arms high, ran her fingers through her hair, and yawned with pleasure. She was very happy.

Ever south, we followed the beautiful white line. I drove slowly. A tender day, a sky like the sea, the sea like the sky. On the left the golden hills, the gold of winter. A day for saying nothing, for admiring lonely trees, sand dunes, and piles of white stones along the road. Camilla's land, Camilla's home, the sea and the desert, the beautiful earth, the immense sky, and far to the north, the moon, still there from the night before.

We reached Laguna before noon. It took me two hours, running in and out of real estate offices and inspecting houses, to find the place we wanted. Anything suited Camilla. Willie now possessed her completely. She didn't care where she lived, so long as she had him. The house I liked was a twin-gabled place, with a white picket fence around it, not fifty yards from the shore. The backyard was a bed of white sand. It was well furnished, full of bright curtains and water-colors. I liked it best because of that one room upstairs. It faced the sea. I could put my typewriter at the window, and I could work. Ah man, I could do a lot of work at that window. I could just look out beyond that window and it would come, and merely looking at that room I was restless, and I saw sentence after sentence marching across the page.

When I came downstairs, Camilla had taken Willie for a walk along the shore. I stood at the back door and watched them, a quarter of a mile away. I could see Camilla bent over, clapping her hands, and then running, with Willie tumbling after her. But I couldn't actually see Willie, he was so small and he blended so perfectly with the white sand. I went inside. On the kitchen table lay Camilla's purse. I opened it, dumped the contents on the table. Two Prince Albert cans of marijuana fell out. I emptied them into the toilet, and threw the cans into the trash box.

Then I went out and sat on the porch steps in the warm sun, watching Camilla and the dog as they made their way back to the house. It was about two o'clock. I had to go back to Los Angeles, pack my stuff, and check out of the hotel. It would take five hours. I gave Camilla money to buy food and the house things we needed. When I left she was lying on her back, her face to the sun. Curled up on her stomach was Willie, sound asleep. I shouted goodbye, let the clutch out, and swung into the main coast highway.

On the way back, loaded down with a typewriter, books, and suitcases, I had a flat tire. Darkness came quickly. It was almost nine o'clock when I pulled into the yard of the beach house. The lights were out. I opened the front door with my key and shouted her name. There was no answer. I turned on all the lights and searched every room, every closet. She was gone. There was no sign of her, or of Willie. I unloaded my things. Perhaps she had taken the dog for another walk. But I was deceiving myself. She was gone. By midnight I doubted that she would return, and by one o'clock I was convinced she wouldn't. I looked again for some note, some message. There was no trace of her. It was as though she had not so much as set foot in that house.

I decided to stay on. The rent was paid for a month, and I wanted to try the room upstairs. That night I slept there, but the next morning I began to hate the place. With her there it was part of a dream; without her, it was a house. I packed my things into the rumble seat and drove back to Los Angeles. When I got back to the hotel, someone had taken my old room during the night. Everything was awry now. I took another room on the main floor, but I didn't like it. Everything was going to pieces. The new room was so strange, so cold, without one memory. When I looked out the window the ground was twenty feet away. No more climbing out the window, no more pebbles against the glass. I set my typewriter in one place and then another. It didn't seem to fit anywhere. Something was wrong, everything was wrong.

I went for a walk through the streets. My God, here I was again, roaming the town. I looked at the faces around me, and I knew mine was like theirs. Faces with the blood drained away, tight faces, worried, lost. Faces like flowers torn from their roots and stuffed into a pretty vase, the colors draining fast. I had to get away from that town.

Chapter Nineteen

My book came out a week later. For a while it was fun. I could walk into department stores and see it among thousands of others, my book, my words, my name, the reason why I was alive. But it was not the kind of fun I got from seeing *The Little Dog Laughed* in Hackmuth's magazine.

That was all gone too. And no word from Camilla, no telegram. I had left her fifteen dollars. I knew it couldn't last more than ten days. I felt she would wire as soon as she was penniless. Camilla and Willie—what had happened to them?

A postcard from Sammy. It was in my box when I got home that afternoon. It read:

> *Dear Mr. Bandini: That Mexican girl is here, and you know how I feel about having women around. If she's your girl you better come and get her because I won't have her hanging around here. Sammy*

The postcard was two days old. I filled the tank with gasoline, threw a copy of my book in the front seat, and started for Sammy's abode in the Mojave Desert.

I got there after midnight. A light shone in the single window of his hut. I knocked and he opened the door. Before speaking, I looked around. He went back to a chair beside a coal-oil lamp, where he picked up a pulp western magazine and went on reading. He did not speak. There was no sign of Camilla.

"Where is she?" I said.

"Damned if I know. She left."

"You mean you kicked her out."

"I can't have her around here. I'm a sick man."

"Where'd she go?"

He jerked his thumb toward the southeast.

"That way, somewhere."

"You mean out in the desert?"

He shook his head. "With the pup," he said. "A little dog. Cute as hell."

"When did she leave?"

"Sunday night," he said.

"Sunday!" I said. "Jesus Christ, man! That was three days ago! Did she have anything to eat with her? Anything to drink."

"Milk," he said. "She had a bottle of milk for the dog."

I went out beyond the clearing of his hut and looked toward the southwest. It was very cold and the moon was high, the stars in lush clusters across the blue dome of the sky. West and south and east spread a desolation of brush, somber Joshua trees, and stumpy hills. I hurried back to the hut. "Come out and show me which way she went," I said. He put down his magazine and pointed to the southeast. "That way," he said.

I tore the magazine out of his hand, grabbed him by the neck and pushed him outside into the night. He was thin and light, and he stumbled about before balancing himself. "Show me," I said. We went to the edge of the clearing and he grumbled that he was a sick man, and that I had no right to push him around. He stood there, straightening his shirt, tugging at his belt. "Show me where she was when you saw her last," I said. He pointed.

"She was just going over that ridge."

I left him standing there and walked out a quarter of a mile to the top of the ridge. It was so cold I pulled my coat around my throat. Under my feet the earth was churning of coarse dark sand and little stones, the basin of some prehistoric sea. Beyond the ridge were other ridges like it, hundreds of them stretching infinitely away. The sandy earth revealed no footstep, no sign that it had ever been trod. I walked on, struggling through the miserable soil that gave slightly and then covered itself with crumbs of grey sand.

After what seemed two miles, I sat on a round white stone and rested. I was perspiring, and yet it was bitterly cold. The moon was dipping toward the north. It must have been after three. I had been walking steadily but slowly in a rambling fashion, still the ridges and mounds continued, stretching away without end, with only cactus and sage and ugly plants I didn't know marking it from the dark horizon.

I remembered road maps of the district. There were no roads, no towns, no human life between here and the other side of the desert, nothing but wasteland for almost a hundred miles. I got up and walked on. I was numb with cold, and yet the sweat poured from me. The greying east brightened, metamorphosed to pink, then red, and then the giant ball of fire rose out of the blackened hills. Across the desolation lay a supreme indifference, the casualness of night and another day, and yet the secret intimacy of those hills, their silent consoling wonder, made death a thing of no great importance. You could die, but the desert would hide the secret of your death, it would remain after you, to cover your memory with ageless wind and heat and cold.

It was no use. How could I search for her? Why should I search for her? What could I bring her but a return to the brutal wilderness that had broken her? I walked back in the dawn, sadly in the dawn. The hills had her now. Let these hills hide her! Let her go back to the loneliness of the intimate hills. Let her live with stones and sky, with the wind blowing her hair to the end. Let her go that way.

The sun was high when I got back to the clearing. Already it was hot. In the doorway of his hut stood Sammy. "Find her?" he asked.

I didn't answer him. I was tired. He watched me a moment, and then he disappeared into the shack. I heard the door being bolted. Far out across the Mojave there arose the shimmer of heat. I made my way up the path to the Ford. In the seat was a copy of my book, my first book. I found a pencil, opened the book to the fly leaf, and wrote:

To Camilla, with love,
Arturo

I carried the book a hundred yards into the desolation, toward the southeast. With all my might I threw it far out in the direction she had gone. Then I got into the car, started the engine, and drove back to Los Angeles.

▲▲▲▲▲

Photo: *Los Angeles Times*

P.S.

Insights,
Interviews
& More . . .

*

About the author

2 Meet John Fante

About the book

4 Letters: John Fante on *Ask the Dust*

13 "Sordid Pictures of Immorality":
Contemporary Takes on *Ask the Dust*

Read on

15 "Fante," a Poem by Charles Bukowski

17 Related Reading (and Viewing)

18 Have You Read?
More by John Fante

Meet John Fante

About the author

Illustration by Salvador Baguez

JOHN FANTE was born in Colorado in 1909. He attended parochial school in Boulder and a Jesuit boarding school (Regis High School) in Denver. He also attended the University of Colorado and Long Beach City College.

Fante began writing in 1929 and published his first short story in *The American Mercury* in 1932. He published numerous stories in the *Atlantic Monthly, The American Mercury, The Saturday Evening Post, Collier's, Esquire,* and *Harper's Bazaar.* His first novel, *Wait Until Spring, Bandini,* was published in 1938. The following year *Ask the Dust* appeared. In 1940 a collection of his short stories, *Dago Red,* was published (now collected in *The Wine of Youth*).

Meanwhile, Fante remained steadily employed as a screenwriter. Some of his credits include *Full of Life, Jeanne Eagels, My Man and I, The Reluctant Saint, Something for a Lonely Man, My Six Loves,* and *Walk on the Wild Side.*

He was stricken with diabetes in 1955. Its complications brought about his blindness in 1978 and (within two years) the amputation of both legs.

* Archival material in P.S. used by permission of Tom Fante and the Estate of John Fante.
** Grateful acknowledgment is made to Stephen Cooper for the kind use of his personal archives.

He continued to write by dictating to his wife, Joyce, and published *Dreams from Bunker Hill* in 1982. He died on May 8, 1983, at the age of seventy-four. ∽

Letters
John Fante on
Ask the Dust

THE FOLLOWING LETTERS, written between 1938 and 1979, detail John Fante's thoughts about *Ask the Dust*—both its creation and reception. Preceding each letter are explanatory notes relating to names and references.

Stackpole Sons published Wait Until Spring, Bandini—*Fante's second completed but first published novel—in October 1938. Within a year another book,* Ask the Dust, *had been finished and published.*

The following is the only letter written by Fante known to date from the time of its composition. Unfortunately, the publisher's plans to "back the book heavily" were upset by heavy financial losses consequent upon losing a copyright infringement case brought on behalf of Adolf Hitler (whose Mein Kampf *Stackpole had published in an unauthorized edition). By 1941 Stackpole Sons was out of business. During this time the Fantes were living in Los Angeles, where Joyce was working on the WPA Federal Writers' Project.*

The "review in the News" would have been in a local Denver newspaper. John Chamberlain's review in Scribner's *compares Fante with James T. Farrell: "Each author writes about an*

John Fante, Roseville, California, 1937

underprivileged Catholic immigrant group
[. . .]. Each brings a searing, disenchanted
understanding to his subject. But Fante believes
in the quintessentializing, 'poetic' technique,
while Farrell uses a mixture of the naturalistic
and the grotesque." It concludes, "All the Bandinis
swing between the polar extremes. Arturo, the
oldest boy, hates himself for being a wop, hates his
freckles, hates the ugly chickens in the back yard,
hates himself when Rosa Pinelli deigns to ignore
him. But Arturo has a deeply hidden family and
race loyalty. He understands his father when
the tormented artisan goes off with the widow
Hildegarde, and he proves that he understands
his mother also when he refuses to tell her of it. In
the end it is Arturo—Arturo with his dog—who
brings the family together again. The end would
have been sentimental in anyone's telling but
Mr. Fante's, but he makes it just right."

[To his cousin Jo Campiglia]
206 No. New Hampshire,
Los Angeles
Nov. 29, 1938

Dearest Jo—

Thanks so much for clinching the review in
the News. As you say, it is a good one and it
should be of some use during the Christmas
season. It was awfully generous of you to work
so hard getting that review—and Edward too:
thank him for me. I thought the review a very
shrewd one, coming as it did from a strong
Catholic: she did a nice job.

The book is going to print this week in
London. Routledge, a very fine and very old
English firm, cabled their acceptance last
week. I don't know what the English edition
will be like, but I imagine no changes will
be made. I should like to have substituted
English hockey or golf for the baseball stuff
in the American, but they were in a rush to
get the book ready for Christmas.

Joyce and I are quite broke but otherwise ▶

Letters *(continued)*

very well and happy. Money is coming, and I hope to start my new novel by the first of the year. Right now I'm writing an outline, and it's a big exasperating job. New book will be called "Ask the Dust on the Road," and the story is in a Los Angeles background (no Hollywood stuff). Story of a girl I once loved who loved someone else, who in turn despised her. Strange story of a beautiful Mexican girl who somehow didn't fit into modern life, took to marijuana, lost her mind, and wandered into the Mojave desert with a little Pekinese dog. It [is] a book like *Human Bondage,* but with humor and wistfulness. I have to have it ready by October next year, which means the writing has to be finished by July.

We are going home for Christmas, and after that our plans are to move somewhere in a place where it is quiet and inexpensive: possibly Monterey.

> Love to everyone,
> Johnnie

Awfully good review in December *Scribner's* by John Chamberlain, considered best American critic.

The Atlantic Monthly *review that Fante mentions to his mother in the next letter was by Ellery Sedgwick. (See the following section of this P.S. for an excerpt of the review.)*

The collaboration with Lynn Root and Frank Fenton that he was hopeful of selling to MGM was in fact made (from a screenplay not by Fante but by S. J. and Laura Perlman) into a movie (The Golden Fleecing*) released in 1940.*

Regarding Fante's statement to his mother that "Joyce and I have been going to mass regularly," Joyce Fante comments simply, "Not true."

> ❝ New book will be called 'Ask the Dust on the Road,' and the story is in a Los Angeles background (no Hollywood stuff). Story of a girl I once loved who loved someone else. ❞

826 South Berendo,
Los Angeles
November 8, 1939

Dearest Mother,

My new book is out today. From reports I get
it has every chance of making a lot of money.
I say this in view of the letters I have had from
my publisher, and from the first reviews,
one of which appears in the December issue
of the *Atlantic Monthly*. Last Friday my
publisher wired me that he was going to back
the book heavily, and I know that the advance
sale is already bigger than my first book. It is—
this new book—a very fine job of printing
and binding, and it looks much better than
the first book. It is displayed in a window
in Beverly Hills, and it is one of the most
attractive jackets I've ever seen. I am sending
you a copy of the book very soon now.

My first book will pick up from this point
too. I know several bookstores have reordered
copies of Bandini, and there is a chance it will
also make some important money. . . .

On the whole everything looks rosy for
the future. A story I wrote with Frank Fenton
and Lynn Root is being considered at Metro.
I think we have a very good chance of selling
it for around six thousand, or two thousand
apiece. We won't have any definite news about
this for a week, but if we do sell the story
Joyce and I will of course come home for
Thanksgiving, and maybe sooner. Another
story of mine is under consideration at
Warner Brothers, and still a third, which is
not finished, will be distributed within a few
days. Something is bound to happen before
Christmas, and perhaps sooner. We hope for
a definite break to the good from now on. I
am in a good position in the publishing world
from now on. I can demand and get big
advances, when I decide to write another ▶

> 66 **The new
> book is displayed
> in a window in
> Beverly Hills, and
> it is one of the
> most attractive
> jackets I've ever
> seen.** 99

> **The success of my new book will naturally open up opportunities for me here in Hollywood.**

> **I had a letter from Paul Reinart asking for a copy of my new book. Priests take a poverty vow and are not permitted to buy such things as books.**

book. In fact, I am sure I can get $2500 advance anytime I ask for it. The success of my new book will naturally open up opportunities for me here in Hollywood, but I shall have to discuss all of that with my agent.

Joyce is well. Today she was down with a bad headache, but that was the first time she has been sick in months. She sent out a batch of poetry to the *Atlantic Monthly,* and it was such good stuff that I'm sure she'll sell a couple of them at least.

I suggest you listen to the radio Sunday night for Joseph Henry Jackson's program from San Francisco. I think he'll review my new book this coming Sunday. If not, he'll cover it the Sunday afterward. The program is either at 6 or 6:30 in the evening. It's a coast-to-coast network program and it should help a great deal, provided he likes the book. I haven't heard from Jackson, and it may be he doesn't like the book, but I think he'll praise it. I enclose a clipping from the *Boulder Camera.* It was sent by Milton Folawn, who is now back in Boulder.

It has begun to rain down here. Today was the first rain of the season, light and cold. I like the change. It has been too hot lately. I am working on a beautiful short story which I know I'm going to sell. Joyce and I have been going to mass regularly these past Sundays. I had a letter from Paul Reinart asking for a copy of my new book. Priests take a poverty vow and are not permitted to buy such things as books. I shall send him one in a few days.

That's all for this time. Love to everyone—
Johnnie

The one or two thousand dollars reported in the next letter to his cousin (for the story The Golden Fleecing *sold to MGM), the successful publication of two novels within thirteen months, and flattering inquiries from publishers*

*about his next project all
combined to make the end of
1939 a moment of financial
comfort and exultant self-
confidence in Fante's career.
But some of the hopes
enumerated above and in
the next letter would be
unfulfilled. No cheap Mercury
Books edition appeared—
doubtless because of
Stackpole's legal troubles. The
"dago story" is unidentified,
but no further stories by Fante
appeared in the* Atlantic Monthly. *By May
1940 he would be reporting himself "worse off
than ever in my life before."*

John Fante at his Malibu ranch, mid-1950s

[To his cousin Jo Campiglia]
Nov 23, 1939

Dear Jo,

I am grateful for your letter, and not surprised
or disappointed that you like Bandini better
than *Ask the Dust,* I think the writing in *Ask
the Dust* is superior to that in Bandini, but
that the story in Bandini was much closer to
me than that in *Ask the Dust.* For that reason
I couldn't possibly make this new book sing
with the lyrical tone of Bandini. The first
book came from my heart; the second from
my head and my—(it starts with p and ends
with k).

The reviews are contradictory. Some
damn the book as obscene; others wildly
praise it. The best review—and it's really a
wonderfully satisfying one—appears in the
December *Atlantic Monthly.* Read it, if you're
interested in my work. That critic really
understood my book, and he has done more
for its sale than any other. The book has
already gone into a second printing, and ▶

we expect a good sale between now and Christmas. Gene Fowler has gone crazy about the book, and is whooping it up everywhere. So too Bill Saroyan, Carey McWilliams, Louis Adamic, and dozens of others.

Incidentally, the Mercury Books (25¢) will shortly bring out a paperbound edition of Bandini. I'm very glad of this, for it will mean close to a million readers. Oh yes— next year Bandini will appear on the New York Stage. Last week I signed papers authorizing a playwright to do it for the stage. Abbott will probably produce it, with Leo Carillo playing the part of Svevo Bandini. Of course all of this is conditioned by a suitable adaptation, but I have a strong hunch it will succeed.

Things are looking better for me. I really think my money problems are finished. The Viking Press has offered me $4000 advance on my new book, which is very tempting, but there are other offers too. I can just about write my own ticket at $300 a month for a year or 18 months. My next book should be the money-maker, which is not important, but critically a big, full book from me that succeeds will put me smacko among writers like Faulkner, Sinclair Lewis, Tom Wolfe. I am a bit worried about doing all of this so soon. What will happen when I'm 40—45—50? I'd rather take it easy.

. . . I'm doing a helluva nice little dago piece for the *Atlantic Monthly*. I'll keep you posted about it. The magazines are crying for my stuff, but they won't give me any guarantee. . . .

Ask the Dust is being considered at Metro and Paramount but I don't think it has a chance. However I may get a job out of it somewhere in town, if I want one. And frankly, I don't. You have no idea how envious and bitter some of the local $2000 per week

> 66 I think the writing in *Ask the Dust* is superior to that in Bandini, but that the story in Bandini was much closer to me than that in *Ask the Dust*. 99

> 66 Things are looking better for me. I can just about write my own ticket at $300 a month for a year or 18 months. 99

"writers" feel toward a man who actually does write and produce a good book. If they'll give me $500 a week and a guarantee of ten weeks I'll take a job. If not, screw them with a bicycle pump.

Tell Grace I'll have money for her soon. I am glad you like Joyce. Of course she love[s] all of us very much. Love to Ralph and your mother and everyone.

johnnie

> **If they'll give me $500 a week and a guarantee of ten weeks I'll take a job. If not, screw them with a bicycle pump.**

Poet/novelist Charles Bukowski (1920–1994) wrote to Fante requesting information for the introduction Bukowski was writing for a new edition of Ask the Dust. *In the letter Bukowski also sought advice about his screenplay for the autobiographical* Barfly, *which would be made into a 1987 film starring Mickey Rourke and Faye Dunaway.*

Fante addressed his response to "Hank" (Bukowski's nickname).

[To Charles Bukowski]
February 6, 1979

Dear Hank:

I usually charge a standard rate of $100 per page for questionnaire letters such as yours, but in view of your responsibility for a good preface I am canceling the usual fee and answering all questions free of charge.

1. *Ask the Dust* was written in 1938.
2. It was published in 1939.
3. I wrote it in an apartment in the 800 block south on Berendo Street.
4. I was living in Los Angeles when it was published.
5. I lived in the Alta Vista Hotel on Bunker Hill in 1934–35. I wrote only fragments during that time—short stories for ▶

The American Mercury. I never had the leisure to involve myself in a novel due to the pressure of paying rent, which was $6 a week—a crushing burden. My back is still bent beneath the weight of that dreadful chore.

Your French director who stands over your shoulder measuring the screenplay at one minute per page sounds like a kook to me. It seems to me that subject matter determines style and time. Maybe you might want to break some rules, maybe write a flashback within the scene. How the hell can you reduce something that lengthy within the confines of the Frenchman's strictures? No. You need limitless horizons and distances. You cannot be bound to the Frenchman's rules. You are the writer, so write a unique, an unorthodox screenplay.

Regards ⌐

❝ Your French director who stands over your shoulder measuring the screenplay at one minute per page sounds like a kook to me. ❞

"Sordid Pictures of Immorality"
Contemporary Takes on *Ask the Dust*

"*Ask the Dust* realizes to the full the quizzical wonder inherent in Saroyan's fragmentary writings, and recognizes the cruelty of man's lot besides. . . . The love of Camilla for Sammy and her disintegration when it is not accepted would start tears from a stone. Fante must have lived this out at some time. And now that he has written his Werther, let us hope fervently he can get on to another Faust."
—*Atlantic Monthly*

"This is a strange novel, one which is most emphatically *not* recommended for reading by the young, or even by the old who dislike sordid pictures of immorality. . . . Yet in many ways it is quite an extraordinary piece of work, and a very Catholic piece of work at that."
—*Commonweal*

"*Ask the Dust* is a sharp and perceptive study of the mind of a boy trying to grow older, a young chap with talent exposed to the conflicting currents of today's society, upset by his own still not-quite-Americanism and his wish that he was a part of the great world he still doesn't quite understand. Arturo will give you a sharp pain in the neck more than once, but if you can remember your own youth at all you'll understand him. And you'll like him, in spite of himself, and be sorry for him. It is hard to see how Mr. Fante could have accomplished more than that."
—*San Francisco Chronicle*

"[T]his new book carries considerable impact and, despite so much that is painful, ▶

> 66 'Fante must have lived this out at some time. And now that he has written his Werther, let us hope fervently he can get on to another Faust.' 99

About the book

"Sordid Pictures of Immorality" *(continued)*

contemptible, ugly in its subject matter, it leaves the reader in a state of speculation and interest. What will this young author's next book be like? He has a quite unexpected sense of humor and any one who could write as he does here of the earthquake or of Camilla with her new dog or of Vera's visit to the hero's room is a man of mark. But meanwhile the reader in search of sweetness and light is warned." —*Books*

66 Any one who could write as he does here of the earthquake is a man of mark. 99

"Fante," a Poem by Charles Bukowski

from Betting on the Muse: Poems & Stories

John Fante, late 1960s

every now and then it comes back to
me,
him in bed there, blind,
being slowly chopped away,
the little bulldog.
the nurses passing through, pulling
at curtains, blinds, sheets.
seeing if he was still alive.
the Colorado Kid.
the courage of the *American
Mercury*.
Mencken's Catholic bad boy.
gone Hollywood.
and tossed up on shore.
being chopped away.
chop, chop, chop.
until he was gone.

he never knew he would be
famous.
i wonder if he would have given
a damn.
i think he would have. ▶

"Fante," a Poem by Charles Bukowski
(continued)

John, you're big time now.
you've entered the Books of
Forever
right there with Dostoevsky,
Tolstoy, and your boy
Sherwood Anderson

I told you.

and you said, "you wouldn't
shit an old blind man,
would you?"
ah, no need for that,
bulldog. ∿

Related Reading (and Viewing)

FULL OF LIFE: A BIOGRAPHY OF JOHN FANTE,
by Stephen Cooper

"By bringing together his life and work for the first time with such clarity of purpose, Stephen Cooper presents a remarkable gift to innumerable fans of Fante's work."
—*Los Angeles Times*

"Fante would have loved this book, unless of course people wind up reading it instead of his fiction, in which case he'd have decked somebody."   —*San Francisco Chronicle*

A SAD FLOWER IN THE SAND,
a film documentary by Jan Louter

Available from Viewpoint Productions, Amsterdam. Contact Valerie Schuit at E.info@viewpointdocs.com or go to www.viewpointdocs.com.

JOHN FANTE: OUTLINE OF A WRITER,
a film documentary by Giovanna DiLello

Available from Cooperativa Rosabella, Pescara, Italy. Contact Cooperativa Rosabella at gdlscriba@tin.it.

Have You Read?
More by John Fante

Excerpts from His Novels

WAIT UNTIL SPRING, BANDINI

He came along, kicking the snow. Here was a disgusted man. His name was Svevo Bandini, and he lived three blocks down that street. He was cold and there were holes in his shoes. That morning he had patched the holes on the inside with pieces of cardboard from a macaroni box. The macaroni in that box was not paid for. He had thought of that as he placed the cardboard inside his shoes.

"Excellent portraiture and a story that holds one's interest to the last page distinguish this novel."   —*New York Times*

1933 WAS A BAD YEAR

It was a bad one, the Winter of 1933. Wading home that night through flames of snow, my toes burning, my eyes on fire, the snow swirling around me like a flock of angry nuns, I stopped dead in my tracks. The time had come to take stock. Fair weather or foul, certain forces in the world were at work trying to destroy me.

"*1933* . . . is stunningly realistic and fuelled by rage at the social inequalities of life in America. It is short, precise, and unforgettable."
                    —*Time Out*

*One night last September my brother phoned
from San Elmo to report that Mama and Papa
were again talking about divorce.*

"So what else is new?"

"This time it's for real," Mario said.

*Nicholas and Maria Molise had been
married for fifty-one years, and though it
had been a wretched relationship from the
beginning, held together by the relentless
Catholicism of my mother who punished her
husband with exasperating tolerance of his
selfishness and contempt, it now seemed utter
madness for these old people to leave each other
at such a late time in their lives, for my mother
was seventy-four and my father two years older.*

"In my view, [Fante] wrote better of the Italians
of California than Saroyan did of the Armenians,
but without the folksy sentimentality that
eventually made Saroyan popular. . . . In
The Brotherhood of the Grape he . . . gives us a
wonderful picture of small-town Italian life."
        —Larry McMurtry, *Washington Post*

Have You Read? *(continued)*

FULL OF LIFE

*It was a large house because we were people with
big plans. The first was already there, a mound
at her waist, a thing of lambent movement,
slithering and squirming like a ball of serpents.
In the quiet hours before midnight I lay with my
ear to the place and heard the trickling as from a
spring, the gurgles and sucks and splashings.*

*I said, "It certainly behaves like the male of
the species."*

"Not necessarily."

"No female kicks that much."

"[A] witty and charming account of a man's
adjustment to his wife's pregnancy."
—*New York Herald Tribune Book Review*

"*Full of Life* is touching as well as funny,
neither wise-cracking nor ponderous.
Not everybody could live on that level of
emotional velocity, but the Fantes seem
built for it."   —*New York Times*

My first collision with fame was hardly memorable. I was a busboy at Marx's Deli. The year was 1934. The place was Third and Hill, Los Angeles. I was twenty-one years old, living in a world bounded on the west by Bunker Hill, on the east by Los Angeles Street, on the south by Pershing Square, and on the north by Civic Center. I was a busboy nonpareil, with great verve and style for the profession, and though I was dreadfully underpaid (one dollar a day plus meals) I attracted considerable attention as I whirled from table to table, balancing a tray on one hand, and eliciting smiles from my customers. I had something else beside a waiter's skill to offer my patrons, for I was also a writer. . . .

"[Fante's] last work . . . a mordantly funny look at life as a 'Hollywood whore.' "

—*The Guardian* (London)

Have You Read? *(continued)*

THE ROAD TO LOS ANGELES

*I had a lot of jobs in Los Angeles Harbor because
our family was poor and my father was dead.
My first job was ditchdigging a short time after
I graduated from high school. Every night I
couldn't sleep from the pain in my back. We
were digging an excavation in an empty lot,
there wasn't any shade, the sun came straight
from a cloudless sky, and I was down in that
hole digging with two huskies who dug with
a love for it, always laughing and telling jokes,
laughing and smoking bitter tobacco.*

"[*The Road to Los Angeles*] wasn't published
until 1985 when it was found among the
author's papers, two years after his death. It
has come to be regarded as something of a
lost classic." —*The Observer* (London)

Other Works and Collections

THE JOHN FANTE READER,
edited by Stephen Cooper

The John Fante Reader includes excerpts from
Fante's novels and stories along with never-
before-published letters.

"Either the work of John Fante . . . is
unknown to you or it is unforgettable. He
was not the kind of writer to leave room in
between. . . . *The John Fante Reader* is poised
to win him a well-deserved place in the
mainstream." —Janet Maslin, *New York Times*

JOHN FANTE: SELECTED LETTERS 1932–1981, edited by Seamus Cooney

Fante's captivating letters trace his emergence from poverty to life as a Hollywood screenwriter. Complemented by many photos and interesting appendices, the book is most distinguished by Fante's letters to his mother—letters in which he is just as apt to lie about church attendance as he is to describe, with peculiar candor, skinny-dipping with a girlfriend.

THE BIG HUNGER: STORIES 1932–1959

Here are eighteen stories collected for the first time, among them a number of "intelligent and meaningful tales of the immigrant experience" (*Publishers Weekly*).

"Each story seems a chiseled jewel, sharply glittering, and without a speck of excess. Fante's gift for dialogue becomes immediately apparent in his opening story, 'Horselaugh on Dibber Lannon,' but shines with something close to perfection in his later story 'Mary Osaka, I Love You.' Set during the outbreak of World War II, it tells of love between a Japanese woman and a Filipino man."
—*San Diego Union-Tribune*

Have You Read? *(continued)*

WEST OF ROME: TWO NOVELLAS

West of Rome's two novellas, "My Dog Stupid" and "The Orgy," fulfill the promise of their rousing titles. The latter novella opens with virtuoso description: "His name was Frank Gagliano, and he did not believe in God. He was that most singular and startling craftsman of the building trade—a left-handed bricklayer. Like my father, Frank came from Torcella Peligna, a cliff-hugging town in the Abruzzi. Lean as a spider, he wore a leather cap and puttees the year around, and he was so bowlegged a dog could lope between his knees without touching them."

THE WINE OF YOUTH: SELECTED STORIES

This new edition of the legendary *Dago Red,* first published in 1940, contains seven new stories, including "A Nun No More" and "My Father's God."

"Here is a book where the author's talent lies over each page bright as sunlight on a fresh green lawn."
—*New York Times* (reviewing *Dago Red*)

Don't miss the next book by your favorite author. Sign up now for AuthorTracker by visiting www.AuthorTracker.com.